"*Marriage isn't something to be taken lightly,*"

Jamie said. "Something happens to a couple when they marry. . .even when it's only a marriage of convenience. Something spiritual. I know you don't agree with me, but we're both going to be affected by this. I can't shake the feeling that deep down we're going to regret this someday."

"We aren't going to share a physical relationship," Rich reminded her.

"I know all that," she argued, "but it doesn't change what I feel."

Her hand was trembling in his, and he knew from the way her voice dipped and rose that she was close to tears. "Do you want to call the whole thing off?" he asked.

"That's the crazy part," she said, trying hard to disguise her dismay. "I want this marriage and our child more than I've ever wanted anything in my life."

"So do I," he admitted. "So do I."

Dear Reader,

Welcome to Silhouette **Special Edition** . . . welcome to romance. Each month, Silhouette **Special Edition** publishes six novels with you in mind—stories of love and life, tales that you can identify with—romance with that little "something special" added in.

And this month has some wonderful stories in store for you. Lindsay McKenna's *One Man's War* continues her saga that is set in Vietnam during the sixties— MOMENTS OF GLORY. These powerful tales will capture you from the first page until the last! And we have an exciting debut this month—Debbie Macomber begins her new series, THOSE MANNING MEN. Don't miss the first book—*Marriage of Inconvenience*— Rich and Jamie's story.

Rounding out March are more stories by some of your favorite authors: Mary Curtis, Erica Spindler, Pamela Toth and Pat Warren. It's a wonderful month for love!

In each Silhouette **Special Edition** novel, we're dedicated to bringing you the romances that you dream about—stories that will delight as well as bring a tear to the eye. And that's what Silhouette **Special Edition** is all about—special books by special authors for special readers!

I hope you enjoy this book and all of the stories to come!

Sincerely,

Tara Gavin
Senior Editor
Silhouette Books

DEBBIE MACOMBER
Marriage of Inconvenience

Silhouette Special Edition

Published by Silhouette Books New York

America's Publisher of Contemporary Romance

To Yakima's Iron Maidens:
Cheryl Nixon, Ellen Bartelli, Joyce Falon,
Jill Seshiki, Faye and Victoria Ives

SILHOUETTE BOOKS
300 East 42nd St., New York, N.Y. 10017

MARRIAGE OF INCONVENIENCE

Copyright © 1992 by Debbie Macomber

ISBN: 0-373-09732-8

First Silhouette Books printing March 1992

All the characters in this book have no existence outside the imagination of the author and have no relation whatsoever to anyone bearing the same name or names. They are not even distantly inspired by any individual known or unknown to the author, and all incidents are pure invention.

®: Trademark used under license and registered in the United States Patent and Trademark Office and in other countries.

Printed in the U.S.A.

Books by Debbie Macomber

DEBBIE MACOMBER

hails from the state of Washington. As a busy wife and mother of four, she strives to keep her family healthy and happy. As the prolific author of dozens of bestselling romance novels, she strives to keep her readers happy with each new book she writes.

Marriage of Inconvenience kicks off a new trilogy chronicling the love lives of "Those Manning Men," the delightful brothers of the Manning sisters, Taylor and Christy.

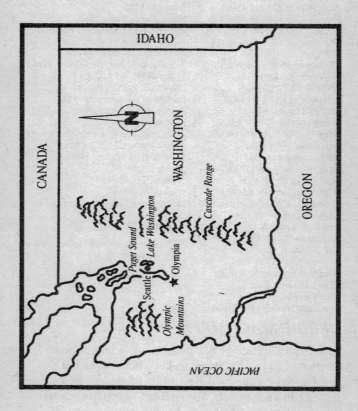

Chapter One

"I'm so stupid," Jamie Warren wailed, carelessly tossing the crumpled tissue over her right shoulder. Rich Manning, who was sitting across the kitchen table from her, handed her a fresh one. "I trusted Tony, and he's nothing more than a . . . jerk."

She yanked the tissue from Rich's hand and ingloriously blew her nose. This tissue took the same path of the one before it. "I feel like the biggest fool who ever lived."

"It's Tony who's the fool."

"Oh, right. Then why am I the one sitting here crying my eyes out?" Jamie really didn't expect him to answer. Contacting Rich at an ungodly hour, sobbing out her tale of woe, hadn't been her most brilliant move, but she needed to talk to someone and he was the first person who'd popped into her mind.

Rich was the type of friend she felt comfortable contacting in the middle of the night. They'd been close ever since they'd worked together on their yearbook in high school. Although they didn't see one another often, Jamie had always considered their relationship special.

"At least crying's better than getting drunk, which is what I did when I found out Pamela was two-timing me," Rich admitted with a wry twist of his mouth. He stood abruptly and poured them both a fresh cup of coffee.

"I take it you haven't seen her since."

"Sure, I have. I wouldn't want her to think I was jealous."

Despite everything, Jamie laughed. "You're still dating her? Even after you learned she was seeing someone behind your back?"

Rich gave a nonchalant shrug as though the entire matter were of little consequence, something Jamie knew not to be the case. He'd been devastated and wore a cavalier facade. He might have fooled everyone else, but Jamie knew him too well to be duped. His flippant attitude couldn't camouflage the piercing pain.

"I took her to a movie a couple of times," Rich continued, "played it cool, that sort of thing. But as far as I'm concerned, it was over the minute I heard about the other guy."

"It's over with me and Tony, too," Jamie murmured. Just saying the words produced a painful tightening in her chest. She was truly in love with Tony and had been for nearly a year. They'd even talked about getting married and raising a family together. Jamie wanted children so badly. The weekend before, they had gone shopping for engagement rings. Her mother was crazy about him, claiming that since Jamie had post-poned getting married until after she'd turned thirty, then waiting for a man like Tony Sanchez had been time well spent. Even her mother had been fooled.

"You're sure the baby is his?" Rich asked, reaching for her hand and squeezing gently. "The woman could be stirring up trouble."

"He didn't bother to deny it." In the beginning, Jamie had hoped for that herself. She'd searched Tony's face, waiting, praying it was all some sick joke. His beautiful dark eyes had brightened defensively, then gradually the regret, the doubt had showed, and he'd slowly slid his gaze away from hers. It had been a mistake, he'd told her, a momentary slip in good judgment. A one-night fling that meant nothing. He felt terrible about it and promised nothing like this would ever happen again.

Tony was cheating on her before they were married, and Jamie didn't need a crystal ball to figure out the pattern was sure to continue.

"This isn't the first time," she admitted, biting hard into her lower lip to control the trembling. "Marge, in New Accounts, casually mentioned seeing Tony with a blonde a month or so ago. He'd told me he was out of town and I . . . I was sure it was just a case of mistaken identity. I should have known then."

"Don't be so hard on yourself," Rich said, bending forward to brush a wisp of dark brown hair from her temple. "There were plenty of signs Pamela was play-ing me for a fool, too, but I was so taken with her . . ."

"Bust line. You always were a breast man."

"That's probably the reason I never dated you," he countered, grinning.

Jamie smiled. The joke was an old one between them. When they'd first been assigned to work together on the yearbook, Rich had been a popular football player and she'd been a nondescript bookworm. They'd clashed in every conceivable way and fought like crazy. One day, after a particularly nasty confrontation, she'd shouted that if she had a bigger bust, he might listen to reason. Rich had gone speechless, then he'd started to laugh. The laughter had broken the ice between them and they'd been friends ever since. The very best of friends.

"I hear there's help in the form of surgery," he teased, leveling his gaze at her chest.

"Oh, honestly." Her breasts weren't that small, but the banter was comfortable and easy between them. It helped her to focus on something other than what a mistake Tony had turned out to be. She'd wasted an entire year of her life on him. An entire year!

Rich reached for his coffee, then leaned back in the chair and sighed, his look dark and brooding. "I'm beginning to wonder if anyone's faithful anymore."

"I'm the last person you should be asking that." She relaxed against the rail-back chair, the coffee mug poised in front of her mouth. She didn't blame Rich for having his doubts. Relationships seemed to be going down the tube these days. Friends, whose marriages had seemed secure and healthy, were divorcing. Affairs seemed rampant at the bank. Casual sex. Jamie was sick of it all.

"When Mark Brooks cheated on my sister Taylor, she upped and accepted that teaching position in another state," Rich went on to say. "You know, I never much liked Mark. From the first I sensed there was something about him. I wish now I'd said something to Taylor."

"I felt so bad for her."

"The whole family was worried about her. Then she moved all the way to the backwoods of Montana and within a few months married Russ Palmer. Everyone was convinced she'd made a terrible mistake, marrying a cowpoke on the rebound, but I've never seen her happier. And now Christy's married to Cody Franklin."

"Christy's married to whom?"

"The Custer County sheriff. She's living in Montana now, too."

"But I thought she was engaged to James Wilkens. Good grief, I was at her engagement party no more than three months ago."

"It's a long story, but James is out of the picture now."

"Christy dumped James?" It was hard to believe. Jamie had assumed the two were perfect for one another. They'd appeared to be the ideal couple at the engagement party, sipping champagne and discussing wedding dates with their families.

Rich chuckled, the sound heavy with his amusement. "If you're surprised at that, wait until you hear this. While Christy was engaged to James, she was *married* to Cody."

Jamie was flabbergasted. She didn't know Rich's youngest sister well, but she would never have believed Christy was the type to do anything so underhanded. "I am surprised."

"There were mitigating circumstances and it's not as bad as it sounds, but Christy is yet another instance of how fickle a woman's heart can be."

"A woman's heart?" Jamie protested. "Men are notoriously untrustworthy—they always have been."

It looked as though Rich wanted to argue with her. He straightened and pressed his elbows against the table, then apparently thought better of it. Sighing, he drank down the last of his coffee. "I'm beginning to doubt that commitment means anything these days."

"I hate to be so cynical, but I share your doubts."

Standing, Rich delivered the mug to the kitchen sink. "Are you going to be able to sleep now?"

Jamie nodded, although she was convinced she wouldn't. However, she'd disrupted Rich enough for one night, and didn't want to keep him any longer.

"Liar," he whispered softly.

Jamie smiled and stood. He slipped his arms around her and squeezed gently, as though to absorb her pain. It felt good to be held. Rich's comfort was like slipping into a hot bath after being stranded in a December snowstorm.

"You're going to get through this."

"I know," she whispered. But she hadn't been nearly as confident of that until she'd talked to Rich. How fortunate she was to have him for her friend. "We both will," she added.

A ragged sigh rumbled through Rich's chest. "Don't you wish life could be as uncomplicated now as it was in high school?"

The remark gave Jamie cause to think. "No," she said, then laughed. "I was painfully shy back then."

"Shy?" Rich argued, releasing her enough to cast her a challenging look with his deep blue eyes. "You were a lot of things, Jamie Warren, but *shy* wasn't one of them."

"Maybe not with you."

"I wish you had been, then you might have done things my way without so much arguing."

"You're still upset I didn't use your picture on the sports page, aren't you? We've been out of high school for nearly thirteen years and you haven't forgiven me for using the shot of Josh McGinnes."

Rich chuckled. "I could be upset, but I'm willing to let bygones be bygones."

"I'm glad to hear it." She led the way through her condo and paused at the front door. Her look sobered. "I really am grateful you came."

"Call if you need me?"

She nodded. The worst of it was over. She would pick up the pieces of her life and start again, a little less trusting and a whole lot more weary.

For no particular reason, the image of Jamie Warren's tear-streaked face drifted into Rich's mind two months later. He'd been sitting at his desk looking over some figures when he remembered her lonely plight. It was as if their conversation had taken place just the night before. He'd talked to her two or three times over the holidays, and she had sounded good. Downright cheerful. In a hell of a lot better spirits than he'd been lately.

She hadn't made any attempt to fool him. Tony had hurt her badly. From what she'd said, he'd made several attempts to get back into her good graces, but it was over. It was plain to Rich that Tony Sanchez didn't really know Jamie Warren. The woman was stubborn enough to impress a mule. Once she set her mind to something, that was it. On the outside she appeared docile and submissive, but Rich had bumped against the stubborn streak of hers himself a time or two and had come away bruised and battered.

It irritated Rich that Jamie had never married. He had fully expected her to have a passel of kids by this time in their lives. She'd always loved children.

Most men, Rich realized, passed Jamie over with little more than a glance. That irritated him even more.

The problem, if he could even call it that, was that she didn't possess the looks of a beauty queen. She wasn't plain, nor was she unappealing. She was just—he hated to admit it—ordinary. Generally, there was one thing or another that stood out in a woman. Not that Rich had given the matter much thought, but it seemed to him that was often the case. Some had eyes that could pierce a man's soul. Jamie had brown eyes. Regular brown eyes. Not deep or brooding or anything else, just plain brown eyes. They were pretty eyes. Nice, but average.

She was only five-five, he'd guess, and a little on the thin side. In giving the matter some consideration, Rich realized there didn't seem to be a distinguishing curve on her. Not her hips, and certainly not her breasts. He could be mistaken of course, but he hadn't looked at her in that way...to be honest, he'd never looked at her any way but as a friend.

She simply didn't have a body that would stop traffic. An ordinary-looking woman with curves, well that was another story entirely. Rich knew his kind well, and he hated like the dickens to admit something so derogatory about his fellowman, but he felt it was true.

What few realized, what few took the time to see, was Jamie's warm heart and generous spirit. He'd never known a more giving woman. What she'd said about her being painfully shy was true, even though he'd denied it. Yet she had spunk and spirit. Enough to stand up to him, which was no easy thing.

Levering his hands against the edge of the desk, Rich rolled back his chair and headed down the hallway with rare determination.

"Bill," he said, striding purposefully into the doorway of the Boeing office. "Have you got a minute?"

"Sure. What's up?"

Rich had never played the role of matchmaker, and he wasn't exactly sure where to start. "There's someone I want you to meet."

"Oh." Bill didn't look overly enthusiastic.

"A friend of mine."

"Widowed or divorced?"

"Single."

Bill's brows arched toward his receding hairline. "You mean a leftover girl."

Rich wasn't comfortable thinking of Jamie as leftover, but this wasn't the time to argue the point. "We went to high school together."

"High school? Exactly how old is she?"

"Thirty-one." Her birthday wasn't until April. Both their birthdays were in April. Jamie loved to lord it over him that she was a whole week older.

"She's never been married?" Bill asked, his voice rising suspiciously. "What's the matter with her?"

"Nothing. She's probably one of the nicest people you're ever likely to meet."

Bill reached for his In basket and brought down a file, flipping it open. "I can't tell you how many times friends—" he paused and glanced up "—good friends, have set me up by claiming the girl was one of the nicest people I was ever likely to meet. No thanks, Rich."

"No thanks. You haven't heard anything about her."

"I've heard enough."

"What's the matter with you?" It was difficult keeping the irritation out of his voice. Bill was thirty-five and twenty pounds overweight, not to mention with a receding hairline. Frankly, Rich didn't think his friend had the right to be so damn choosy.

"Nothing's wrong with me."

"I thought you wanted to remarry."

"I do. Someday, when I find the right woman."

"You might well be passing her over right now," Rich argued. "I'm not going to lie to you—no one's awarded her a tiara, but she's not ugly, if that's what concerns you."

"Why don't you take her out yourself, then?"

The question took Rich by surprise. "Well, because . . . because it would be like dating one of my sisters."

Bill released an impatient sigh. "Why haven't you mentioned her before now?"

"She was involved with someone else."

Bill emphatically shook his head. "Forget it. You're a good friend and all that, but I've been set up too many times in the past couple of years. Frankly, your friend has everything I want to avoid in a woman. She's over thirty and never been married. That tells me something. It doesn't help that she's just out of another relationship, either. I'm sorry, Rich, really I am, but I'm not interested."

Rich found Bill's attitude downright insulting. Before he could stop himself, long before he could analyze his actions, he reached for his wallet.

"What are you doing?" Bill wanted to know, when Rich pulled out two tickets.

"These are tickets for the Seahawks play-off game against Denver. The scalpers are getting a hundred bucks each for these. If you agree to call Jamie for a date, they're yours." His older brother would have his hide for this, but Rich would deal with Jason later.

Bill's eyes rounded incredulously. "You mean you're willing to give me two tickets to the Seahawks play-off game if I agree to wine and dine your friend?"

"You got it."

Even then Bill hesitated. "One date?"

"One date." But once his fellow engineer had the opportunity to know Jamie, he'd realize what a diamond in the rough she was. Within a few weeks, Bill would be looking for ways to repay him for this good turn. Rich would keep that thought in mind when he told Jason he'd *given* away their play-off tickets.

"Someplace nice, too. No pizza in a bowling alley for Jamie, understand?"

Bill's hand closed over the tickets. "Dinner at the Space Needle followed by an evening at the ballet."

"Good. Just don't ever let Jamie know about this."

Bill laughed. "Do I look that stupid?"

To Rich's way of thinking, any man who would turn down the opportunity to meet Jamie Warren wasn't exactly a candidate for Mensa.

"Here's her phone number," he said, writing it on a slip of paper. "I'll give her a call, clear the way, but the rest is up to you."

"No problem," Bill said, pocketing the sought-after tickets. "I've done this a hundred times."

Rich felt downright noble as he returned to his own office. Jamie was one hell of a woman and it was about time someone realized as much. Bill Hastings wasn't nearly good enough for her, but he was an amiable sort of guy. Without too much trouble Rich could picture

Bill and Jamie a few years down the road raising two or three kids.

He felt good about that, better than he had in quite some time.

That evening, Rich stopped off at Jason's apartment and was relieved to find his brother was out. The longer he delayed telling him what had become of the play-off tickets, the better.

After killing the dinner hour at his own apartment, Rich decided to drive over to Jamie's. He rang the doorbell and waited. It hadn't occurred to him that she might not be home. He was ready to turn away when he heard some activity on the other side.

"Who is it?"

"The big bad wolf."

The sound of her soft laugh was followed by the turning click of the lock. She opened the door and stepped aside. Apparently he'd gotten her out of the bathtub. She had hastily donned a thick white terry-cloth robe that clung to her hips.

"Rich," she said, surprise elevating her voice, "what are you doing here?" As she spoke, she wrapped the tie around her waist, efficiently knotting it.

Rich was having trouble taking his eyes off the creamy smooth skin of her upper thigh to answer right away. His gaze followed a natural progression downward, and he was momentarily astounded to note what long shapely legs she had. Funny, he'd never noticed them before. He grinned, thinking Bill was in for more of a surprise than he realized.

"Don't let me detain you," he said casually, walking into her kitchen. "I'll make myself at home while you finish your bath."

"I'm just about done."

"Take your time," he called out. He stepped into the kitchen, stuck his head inside the refrigerator and brought out an apple. He was polishing it against his shirt when Jamie walked in. As best he could tell, she'd run a brush through her hair and donned slippers. But that was it. The robe rode over her slender hips like a second skin.

"Do you have any plans tonight?" Generally he himself went out on Fridays, but there wasn't anything he was particularly keen on doing this week.

"What have you got in mind?"

"A movie. I'll even let you choose."

"I suppose you're going to make me pay my own way?"

"I might." He grinned, pleased he'd come up with the idea. The suggestion they attend a movie had come as much of a revelation to him as it obviously was to Jamie. As much a surprise as offering Bill the play-off tickets.

Actually, now that he thought about it, it was a damn good idea. This way he could lead into the subject of Bill in a natural, unstilted way while in a casual setting. The last thing he wanted Jamie to think was that he'd prearranged everything.

The movie turned out to be a stroke of genius, Rich decided later. He'd always enjoyed Jamie's company and never more so than now. An evening with her, without the games and the pretense of taking out someone new, was exactly what he needed to settle his nerves. He didn't like to say much, particularly to his family, but Pamela had hurt him. Bad. He didn't trust his judgement when it came to women. Oh, he dated. Often. But he'd grown weary of all the games. Pamela hadn't just broken his heart—the damage she'd inflicted went far deeper. She'd caused him to doubt himself.

Rich pulled into a movie complex in the Seattle suburbs, close to Jamie's condominium. He bought their tickets, but she insisted on buying the popcorn and the chocolate-covered raisins.

He was just thinking how nice it was to be with a woman who wasn't constantly worrying about her weight when she leaned over and whispered, "You ate more than your share of the raisins."

"Do you want me to buy you more?"

"No, just remember you owe me."

It wasn't until several minutes later when Rich realized the film was actually quite serious and he had no reason to be grinning the way he was.

"We don't do this often enough," Rich said on the way out the door. He meant it, too. He'd been at loose ends the last several months, but hadn't thought about contacting Jamie.

"No, we don't," she agreed, buttoning up her coat. She wore jeans and a pale pink sweater. The color looked good on her. He was about to say as much when he remembered the reason for his impromptu visit.

"How about a cup of coffee?" he suggested, linking his arm through hers. There was a coffee shop in the same complex as the theater, and he steered them in that direction.

He waited until they were seated and looking over the menu before he casually brought up Bill's name. "There's someone at work I'd like you to meet."

Jamie didn't raise her eyes from the menu. "Who?"

"Bill Hastings. You'll like him."

"Is he tall, dark and handsome?"

"Yes. No and no."

"Sounds like my kind of man," Jamie joked, setting aside the menu. The waitress automatically filled the ceramic mugs with coffee. "From everything I've heard it's best to avoid the handsome ones."

"Oh?" He already knew what was coming. He wasn't conceited, but Rich knew he was easy on the eyes. A fact that hadn't gone unnoticed from the time he was in his early teens. Rich had never lacked for female attention, some he sought and some he didn't.

"The handsome ones aren't to be trusted," she announced.

"Who says?" Rich demanded, feigning outrage.

"Everyone," Jamie returned without a pause. "They're high on themselves, or so it's been said."

Rich chuckled and, motioning for the waitress, ordered a chef salad, feeling like eating a decent meal for the first time in a good long while. He didn't even complain when Jamie stole his olives, claiming it was the least he could do for hogging the chocolate-covered raisins.

Tuesday morning, Bill strolled into Rich's office, pulled out a chair and plunked himself down. His face was creased with a heavy frown. "It didn't work."

Rich tried to figure out which project Bill was referring to and came up blank. The two were part of an engineering team that was working on a Boeing defense contract. Rich had volunteered for this particular job, knowing it would demand plenty of overtime hours. The challenge was something he needed at this point in his life.

"What do you mean?" he asked Bill.

"She turned me down flat."

Bill couldn't possibly be talking about Jamie. He'd paved the way for him, rolled out the red carpet. He'd even managed to casually drop his name into the conversation two or three times. Just enough to pique her curiosity, but not often enough for her to suspect he was setting the two of them up.

"She turned you down?" Rich echoed, still unable to believe it. "Obviously you didn't try hard enough."

"If I'd tried any harder, I would have been arrested," Bill argued. He rubbed his hand over his forehead.

"What the hell did you say to her?"

"Nothing. I called her Saturday afternoon, just the way you suggested. I mentioned your name right off and told her we worked together and had for several years. I wanted her to feel comfortable talking to me." He hesitated as though he were still trying to figure out what went wrong himself.

"Then what happened?" Rich could feel himself losing patience. He had big bucks invested in this match, and he wasn't about to let Bill off so easily.

"That's just it. Nothing happened. We must have talked for ten or fifteen minutes and you're right about one thing. She sounds nice. Real nice. The more we talked, the more I realized I really wouldn't mind getting to know her better. She mentioned how you two had been on the yearbook staff together.... She even told me a few insider secrets about your glorious football days."

"What the hell were you doing talking about me?" Rich demanded.

"I was establishing common ground."

Rich rubbed his hand over his mouth in an effort to control his irritation. "Go on."

"There's not much to tell. After several minutes I asked her out to dinner. Honest, Rich, I was beginning to look forward to meeting her. I couldn't have been more surprised when she turned me down."

"What did she say?"

"Not much," Bill admitted, his frown deepening. "Just that she'd given up dating and although she was sure I was a perfectly fine gentleman, she wasn't interested."

"You didn't take that sitting down did you?"

"Hell, no. I sent her a dozen roses first thing Monday morning, hoping that would convince her to change her mind. Red roses, expensive ones. I didn't find them in any grocery store, either. These were flower shop roses, top quality."

"And?"

"That didn't do anything, either. She phoned and thanked me, but said she wasn't interested. Said she felt bad I'd gone through the expense of sending her the flowers."

Rich muttered under his breath. Bill was butting heads against that stubborn pride of hers. Rich knew from experience it wouldn't do any good. Clearly she'd made up her mind and nothing was going to change it.

Bill sighed unevenly, as though he'd worked a twenty-hour shift and been informed he had to be back in the office within the next five hours. "You aren't going to make me return the Seahawks play-off tickets, are you?"

Chapter Two

Jamie was sitting at the kitchen table, reading over the application for the adoption agency, when the doorbell rang. One long blast was immediately followed by three short, impatient bursts. By the time she'd stood and walked across the condominium, whoever was on the other side was knocking loudly.

She checked the peephole. Rich. And from the looks of him, he was furious. Unbolting the lock, she opened the door.

Without a word, he marched into the center of her living room, his hands buried deep in the pockets of his full-length winter coat. Damn, but the man was attractive, Jamie noted, not for the first time. Much too handsome for his own good. The irritation flashing from his electric blue eyes only added to his appeal.

"You turned down Bill Hastings's dinner invitation and I want to know why," he demanded without preamble.

Jamie sighed. She should have realized Rich would be upset about that. He'd apparently gone to a good deal of trouble to arrange the date and even more bother trying to conceal it from her. The seemingly impromptu visit Friday night, the movie and even the coffee afterward had all led up to him wanting her to meet his dear friend, Bill Hastings. By the time Rich had finished listing all the man's seemingly limitless virtues, Jamie had been ready to vault to her feet, place her hands over her heart and sing "God Bless America."

To be fair, she had enjoyed talking to Bill. He had seemed cordial enough, and he had sent her the roses, which really were quite lovely. But he hadn't said or done anything that would change her mind. It did seem rather harsh to turn him down sight unseen, but she was saving them both a good deal of trouble and disappointment. Bill seemed to accept her decision with good grace, but that apparently wasn't the case with Rich.

"Well?" Rich demanded. He walked around her sectional as though standing still were impossible and he needed to keep moving. If he didn't stop circling soon, he was going to make her dizzy.

"He sounds very nice."

"The guy's perfect for you," Rich argued, gesturing toward her. "I went to all this trouble to match the two of you up and then you turned him down. I can't believe you refused to even meet him."

"I'm sorry, but I'm just not interested."

"One date," he cried, waving his index finger at her. "What possible harm could come out of one lousy dinner date?"

"None, I'm sure," she returned calmly. "Listen, do you intend to stay long enough to take off your coat, or is this a quick visit to argue with me on your way to someplace else?"

"Are you going to allow Tony to do this to you?" he challenged, disregarding her question. He plowed his fingers through his hair, something he'd done often if the deep grooves along the side of his head were any indication.

"Tony has very little to do with this." Rather than discuss the man who had wounded her so deeply, Jamie moved into the kitchen and automatically poured them tall glasses of iced tea. The action gave her a few minutes to compose her thoughts.

"Obviously Tony has everything to do with this, otherwise you wouldn't have told Bill you'd given up dating. Which, by the way, is the most ridiculous thing I've ever heard." He shucked off his coat and draped it over the back of the kitchen chair.

"Really?" Leaning her hip against the kitchen counter, she added sugar and ice to her glass, then sipped from her tea. Rich ignored the glass she'd poured for him.

"It's not true, is it?"

He glared at her as though he fully expected her to deny everything. Jamie had the feeling if she did, he'd demand a polygraph. She couldn't see any reason to lie about it. "As a matter of fact it is true."

Rich's jaw sagged open as though she'd said something completely and utterly shocking.

"Why?"

"You mean you honestly need to ask?" Jamie asked with a light laugh.

"How can you deny Tony's responsible for this?"

She lifted her shoulders in a light shrug. "In part he is, but this decision isn't solely due to what happened with him. It's just one more disappointment. If anything, I'm grateful I found out what kind of man Tony was *before* we were married."

The timer on her oven dinged, and setting aside her tea, Jamie reached for a pot holder and brought out bubbling chicken potpie. The recipe was one she'd happened upon in a women's magazine and it had sounded delicious. True, the meal was enough to feed a family of four, but she intended to freeze half of it.

"Have you had dinner?" She extended the invitation casually as she set the steaming pie on top of the stove to cool.

"No," Rich answered starkly. "I'm not hungry."

"It seems to me you've lost a few pounds. Have you?"

"I'm not here to discuss my weight," he barked, "which hasn't changed since high school, I might add."

His attitude was slightly defensive, but Jamie decided to ignore it. He had lost weight; she'd noticed it soon after he'd broken off the relationship with Pamela. Jamie had never met the other woman and it was all she could do to think civilly of her. If anyone was ever a fool, it was Rich's former girlfriend.

"You didn't answer my question," Rich said. His voice had lowered several decibels and he seemed less persistent. Jamie fully suspected he'd spent the day stewing over her decision not to date his friend.

"Which question didn't I answer?" she asked, returning the pot holder to the top drawer.

"What made you decide to give up dating?"

"Oh." She pulled out a chair and sat down. Rich followed suit. "Well, it wasn't something I did lightly, trust me. It was a gradual decision made over the past several months, but I honestly feel it's the right one for me. I feel better now than I have in years." She took the time to reassure him with a warm smile. He was frowning at her as though it was all he could do not to stand up and argue. Rich always had been passionate when it came to people he cared about deeply. "I'm nearly thirty-two years old."

"So?"

"So," she said with a laugh, "there aren't many eligible men left for me anymore."

"What about Bill Hastings? He's eligible."

"Divorced, right?"

"Right. But what has that got to do with anything?"

He wasn't going to like her answer, but Jamie wouldn't be anything less than honest. "I've dated plenty of divorced men over the years. My experience may not be like anyone else's, but generally there's a damn good reason their wives left them. If not, they're so traumatized by the divorce that they've become emotional cripples."

"That's ridiculous, and furthermore, it's not fair."

"I'm sure there are plenty of exceptions. I just haven't found any."

"In other words, you wouldn't date Bill because he's divorced."

"Not exactly. It's much more than that. I just don't happen to want to date anyone right now, divorced or not."

"What about single men? You're only thirty-one for heaven's sake. There are plenty of single men out there who would give anything to meet a woman like you."

Jamie had to swallow a sarcastic reply. If there were as many eligible single men as Rich seemed to think there were, then she hadn't met them. "Obviously I haven't had much luck with that group, either," she stated calmly. "I hate to burst your bubble here, but single men aren't all they're cracked up to be either. If a man is in his thirties and not married, there is usually a good reason for it. Besides, single men over thirty are so set in their ways, they have problems adjusting to the natural give-and-take in a healthy relationship."

"That's downright insulting."

"I don't mean for it to be." She stood and reached for two plates. "I'm not going to lie to you and claim Tony had nothing to do with this decision. He hurt me, and it took me several weeks to work through the pain. As strange as it may sound, I'm actually grateful for what Tony taught me. He helped me reach some sound, honest decisions about myself and my life."

"If this no-dating stand of yours is one of them, then I'd do some rethinking, if I were you." Rich opened the silverware drawer and brought out two sets. Without glancing at them, he placed the adoption papers to one side and had the table set by the time she brought over the plates. Jamie couldn't help being pleased that he'd decided to join her for dinner.

"The biggest, and probably most significant realization," she stated while smoothing the napkin across her lap, "was that I like my life just the way it is. I don't need a man to be complete."

Several moments passed before Rich spoke. "That sounds healthy, but to lock the door on any chance of a relationship—"

"I'm not locking the door," she interrupted, eager to correct the impression. "I'm just giving up looking for one. I've wasted years attempting to fulfill the dream of being married and raising children."

Rich took a bite of the chicken potpie and cocked his brows. "Hey, this is good."

"Thank you." She sampled the recipe herself and was pleased with her culinary efforts. Taking the time to cook real meals instead of thoughtlessly throwing something together or succumbing to frozen entrées had been another decision she'd reached. It would sound silly to anyone else, but cooking gave her a feeling of permanence and purpose. She was doing something healthy for herself, and she felt good about it.

"Everything you've said makes damn good sense," Rich admitted reluctantly.

"Don't sound so shocked."

"It's just that I've always pictured you with kids."

"I've got that covered," she said enthusiastically, reaching for the top sheet of the papers Rich had stacked on the other side of the table. "I fully intend to adopt."

"They allow single women to adopt children?" He sounded incredulous.

"I'm just beginning to look into that now. But from what little I've read, I don't think it's going to be easy or anytime soon, especially if I want a newborn."

"Which you do?"

Jamie nodded eagerly. If she was only going to be a mother once, then she wanted as much of the experience as she could have, including midnight feedings, teething and changing diapers. "I have an appointment with a counselor at an adoption agency tomorrow afternoon. I can't remember being more excited about anything."

"I take it you haven't told your mother."

Jamie rolled her eyes at the mere thought. There wasn't any reason to stir up trouble just yet. "It's best that I don't say anything, at least for now. Mom's wonderful, but she'd never understand this."

Rich chuckled and as the laughter drained from his features, his eyes took on a distracted, faraway look. "You know what I have a hard time believing?"

"What?" she asked softly.

"That I'd basically come to the same decision myself. I'm sick to death of the dating game and women whose only interest is getting me into the sack. Lord, I never knew women could be so aggressive."

Intrigued, Jamie could only nod. She would never have believed Rich would experience the same difficulties as she had. For years she'd been looking for him to marry, but had never felt comfortable enough to ask why he hadn't.

"I've spent the better part of ten years looking for a woman who believes love lasts longer than an hour," he added grimly. "As for commitment and honesty, I don't think they exist anymore. If they do, then I can't seem to find anyone who believes in them as strongly as I do. It dawned on me after Pamela cheated on me that I'm a self-reliant adult—and if I never marry, it wouldn't be any great loss."

"That's the same way I feel," Jamie said. "I just never expected that—"

"You did, too," he finished for her.

"Exactly."

They exchanged a look, his deep blue eyes meshed with her plain brown ones, a look wrought with meaning, understanding and empathy. They'd been friends for years and Jamie had never realized how much in common they actually shared.

"I hadn't known it was happening to you, too," she whispered. She felt as though someone were withholding oxygen from her. Everything in the kitchen seemed to fade from view. Everything, that was, except Rich. If anything, his dark good looks came into sharp focus. As she had a thousand times before, Jamie acknowledged what a handsome devil Rich Manning was. But there was so much more there, more than she'd ever noticed before. This was a man of character and strength. A man of substance. He looked older; the years since their high school days had marked their passage. There were wrinkles in his brow. The shadows beneath his eyes were more pronounced and included a few hidden ones in the well-defined angles of his cheeks. On anyone else they would have diminished their appeal, but not Rich. The wrinkles and the shadows were both strangely becoming.

The silence between them stretched to embarrassing proportions. It was Jamie who pulled her eyes away from him—dragged them more aptly described the action, she decided. With a weak smile, she reached for her fork and managed to swallow down a bite of her dinner.

"This is good, isn't it?" she said, making light conversation.

"Excellent." He seemed equally intent on putting their conversation back on an even keel. He attacked his dinner as though he needed to assure himself the chicken was dead.

They chatted for several more minutes, teased one another, exchanged the banter that was so familiar between them. Rich insisted on helping her clean up, but as soon as they were finished, he made his excuses and left.

Jamie felt weak afterward. Weak and trembly as she had the first time she'd stood on the high dive. The feeling wasn't any more comfortable now than it had been all those years ago.

As hard as he tried over the next few days, Rich couldn't forget the look he'd shared with Jamie at her kitchen table on Tuesday evening. He'd tried to define it, garner its significance. It was the type of look long-time lovers exchange. The kind he'd witnessed between Taylor and Russ, as though they had no need for words to say what was in their hearts.

But Jamie and he had never been lovers. To the best of his knowledge they'd never even kissed. Really kissed. A peck on the cheek now and again, if that. A friendship hug perhaps, but that was it. Their relationship had always been strictly platonic. It was the way they both wanted it. Anything else would destroy the special closeness they shared.

Rich shook his head in an effort to clear the disturbing thoughts. Until Tuesday, he'd always viewed Jamie as ordinary. Not anymore.

Still, nothing had changed, not really. At least nothing he could put his finger on. Jamie Warren was the same person she'd always been.

Not so, he corrected. Her eyes had been different.

To think he'd once believed her eyes were an average shade of brown. He'd never seen eyes the precise color of Jamie's. They were a cross between green and brown;

some would call it hazel, he guessed. That night they'd been more green, reminiscent of the mist rising off the moss-covered floor of a rain forest.

But it wasn't her eyes that had intrigued him. It was something far more profound than that. Something far more baffling, too.

His thoughts were interrupted by the phone. Rich reached for the television controller and muted the volume. He didn't know why he'd bothered to turn it on—from habit he guessed. For the past hour he hadn't heard a single word of the local or national news. His thoughts had been tied up analyzing what had happened between him and Jamie.

"Hello," he answered briskly. Pamela sometimes phoned him still, and he braced himself on the off chance it might be her.

"Hi," came the soft feminine voice he recognized immediately as belonging to Jamie.

"Hi, yourself." He felt a bit ill at ease, something he'd never experienced with her. It was as though they hadn't found their stride with one another yet, which was ridiculous. Perhaps he was taking his clue from Jamie. She didn't sound quite like herself; she sounded tense, as if it had taken a good deal of courage for her to contact him. Jamie Warren might be a lot of things, he thought to himself, but a coward wasn't one of them.

"I was just thinking about you." He probably shouldn't have admitted that, but it had slipped out naturally.

"Oh?"

"Yeah, I was going to give you a call later and find out how the appointment went with the adoption agency."

She paused, and he heard her suck in a deep breath. "Actually that was the reason I was calling you. Are you busy?"

"Not really. What do you have in mind?"

"Would it be all right if I stopped by for a few minutes? There's something I need to talk over with you."

"Sure, you're welcome anytime." He glanced around the apartment to see what kind of shape it was in. Not bad. Not especially good, either, but he'd have plenty of time to pick up the newspapers and straighten the cushions.

As it turned out, he had time to wipe down the kitchen countertop, as well, and stick his dirty dishes in the dishwasher. The best meal he'd had in weeks had been the chicken potpie he'd eaten at Jamie's place. He couldn't remember her being such an excellent cook. She certainly seemed full of surprises lately.

Jamie arrived no more than ten minutes after her phone call. She wore jeans and the same pink sweater she'd had on the night they'd gone to the movies. He was about to tell her how nice she looked, but stopped himself. Curiously, his heart stopped, too. Just a little.

"That didn't take long," he said instead.

"No...we only live four or five miles away from each other."

"Yeah." He led the way to the sofa and sat down, resting his ankle on top of his knee and draping his arm along the back. "So what's on your mind?"

Jamie sat down, too, but he noticed that she sat on the very edge of the cushion and rubbed her hands over her thighs as though she were chilled.

Her actions prompted his offer. "Would you like a cup of coffee?"

"Please," she responded eagerly.

Rich couldn't shake the impression that she was thinking of the coffee more as a delaying tactic than any real desire for something to warm her.

It didn't take him long to assemble a pot of coffee. Within a few minutes, he delivered two steaming mugs into the living room. It took him a minute to find two coasters, but once he did, he sat down on a recliner and resumed his relaxed pose.

"How'd the appointment with the adoption agency go?" he asked, when she didn't immediately launch into the reason for the visit.

Her hands cupped the mug and she stared into the dark liquid. "Not very well, I'm afraid. Naturally the agency prefers to place newborns with established families. The waiting list is years long already, and frankly, I don't feel I have all that time to wait."

"I'm sorry to hear that." Rich felt her disappointment keenly. It had obviously been a blow.

"If I'm going to have a child, then I want to be young enough to enjoy her."

"Her?"

"Or him," she amended quickly, briefly glancing his way.

"So what's next?"

For a long time she didn't say anything. Rich might have prompted other people, but he found himself more patient with Jamie. He watched the play of emotions move across her face and tried to read her thoughts. It was impossible to know what she had on her mind, but whatever it was, seemed dark and problematic.

"You're going to think I'm a candidate for intensive counseling when I suggest this."

"Try me."

"I . . . I've made an appointment with my gynecologist. I want to discuss the prospect of being artificially inseminated."

Rich was relieved that his mouth wasn't filled with coffee, otherwise he would have choked himself half to death. "You're going to do *what?*"

Jamie stood abruptly and walked around the back of his recliner and braced her hands against the sides as if she needed to hold on to the barrier between them. "I know it sounds crazy, but I mean to have a child, and if I can't adopt, then this was the best idea I could come up with."

"What about checking with another adoption agency?"

"I did. Five others, and the story's the same. If I want an infant, it will mean years on a waiting list. Two of the agencies wouldn't even talk to me. The others tried to persuade me to become a foster parent with the possibility of adopting at some time in the distant future. I want a baby. Is that so wrong?"

"No," he assured her gently.

"I'm nearly thirty-two years old, and my biological clock is ticking. Not so loud it keeps me awake nights, but loud enough. If I'm going to do this it's got to be soon." Jamie's eyes filled with tears, but she was too proud and too stubborn to let them fall. Her gaze met his without wavering, as though she cursed herself for being honest because it forced her to reveal her deepest inner secrets.

"What about the father?"

"I . . . I'm not sure. I've read everything I could find on the subject, which is admittedly little. From what I understand there's a sperm bank in our area. I don't know what to tell you about it since I haven't been in to see the doctor yet. I'll have more answers once I've had a chance to talk it over with him."

"I see." Rich was having trouble believing they were having this discussion. "You're sure you want to go through with this?" The minute he asked the question, he knew he'd made a mistake.

Steely determination shone from Jamie's eyes. "I mean to do this, Rich, so don't even think of trying to talk me out of it."

Her warning wasn't necessary; Rich knew better. "Are you worried about what people are going to say? Is that what's troubling you?"

She shrugged. "A little. Naturally, the biggest hurdle will be my mother, but I'm not overly worried. It's my life. Besides, she's been after me to have children for years. Of course she'd prefer it if I were married, but I've decided against that." Her gaze skirted to his. She seemed nervous, edgy. Rich couldn't remember Jamie being either. Not ever.

"Something's troubling you."

Briefly she closed her eyes and nodded. "You're just about the best friend I have."

"I'm honored you feel that way."

"I have several close girlfriends. I've been a maid of honor twice and a bridesmaid three times. But when I found out about Tony, it was you I turned to. It was you I felt comfortable enough to wake up in the middle of the night."

"I feel the same way about you."

Her smile was genuine, if not a little shaky. "That pleases me more than you know. We're good friends."

"Good friends," Rich echoed. Good enough for him to hand over two fifty-yard-line play-off tickets on the off chance she might find happiness with Bill Hastings. He'd done it without a pause, willing to do whatever he could for Jamie.

"I'd do just about anything for you," she said, eyeing him closely.

Rich didn't know why he felt that was a leading statement, but he did. The doors were left wide open for him to echo the sentiment. "You're special to me, too. Do you mind telling me exactly where this conversation is leading?"

Jamie came around the chair and sat down. She leaned forward and rubbed her palms together as though she were standing in below-freezing temperatures. She seemed more sure of herself now, less nervous.

"You're such a handsome cuss."

Rich frowned. "What's that got to do with anything?"

"You come from a wonderful family."

That was true enough. "So?"

"You're tall. What I wouldn't give for an extra two inches."

"Jamie, what the hell are you talking about?"

She stood, continued to rub her palms. Once more she positioned herself behind his recliner. "I . . . I was having dinner when it dawned on me exactly what I had decided to undertake. I want a child and because I do, I'm willing to be subjected to heaven only knows what kind of medical procedure. Frankly, I don't care. It's a small sacrifice, and I'm amenable to whatever it takes. The only aspect of this entire scenario is giving birth to a stranger's child. A man I've never met, let alone seen. There are so many unknowns involved. Then it came to me. There was one person, a wonderful man I admire and trust above all others. It didn't make any sense to me to go through all this and give birth to a stranger's baby when . . . when there was someone who was tall, dark and handsome. Someone with excellent chromosomes who might be willing to contribute to this project."

"What are you saying?" Maybe she didn't mean what he thought she meant. Maybe this was all a dream and he'd wake in the morning and have a good laugh over it. Maybe Jamie wasn't far off when she mentioned intensive counseling. There seemed to be a hundred earth-shattering maybes in this. Rich didn't like the answer to a single one of them.

Jamie's gaze met his and she smiled, the softest, sweetest smile he'd ever seen. "I'm asking you to be the sperm donor for my baby."

Chapter Three

"Naturally, I don't expect you to make a decision tonight," Jamie added, walking around the recliner and sitting down once again. She leaned back and crossed her legs, striking a relaxed pose.

Rich frowned. She sounded so casual, so comfortable with the idea once she'd made the suggestion. Mentioning it had demanded a good deal of fortitude, but now that this baby idea was out in the open, she seemed completely at ease.

But Rich was not. His thoughts were in chaos.

"I'm...not sure...what to say," he stammered.

"I don't expect you do. I'm sure the whole thing comes as a shock," she said, and he noted the way her voice dipped softly with regret. "I wish there were some way I could have led up to it with a little more tact, but I couldn't think how to say it other than flat out. I didn't want there to be any room for misunderstanding between us.''

Rich was the one standing now, although he couldn't remember coming to his feet. ''No...this is the best way.'' He paced in front of the coffee table a couple of times, his steps clipped and precise. ''A baby,'' he repeated, needing to hear it aloud for himself. He was waiting for his mind to assimilate exactly what it was Jamie was suggesting. He paused, waiting for a forceful list of objections, but apparently he was too numb to think clearly. Not a single protest came to him. Not even one.

Questions. There were plenty of those. A few doubts and a whole lot of shock, but no real opposition. At least not the way he anticipated there would be. Should be.

''Our baby,'' she added softly, her smile serene, as though she was already pregnant and counting the days before their child's birth.

Her attitude, the calm way she was watching him, unnerved Rich more than anything. He stalked into the kitchen and refilled his coffee mug, although he hadn't taken more than a few sips from the first cup. When he returned, he noticed that Jamie was studying him closely.

''Say something.'' Her confidence seemed to be shaken, and for his own peace of mind, Rich was pleased to see it. She seemed to take the whole matter in stride.

''I don't know what to say,'' he admitted bluntly.

''The whole thing sounds preposterous, doesn't it?''

''Yes.'' He nearly shouted his answer. Preposterous was only the tip of the iceberg. She was talking about creating a new life, one that would forever link them.

"Why is it so ridiculous?"

"Why?" He couldn't believe she'd even ask such a thing. "I'm supposed to father your child. A baby... any baby is a huge responsibility and—"

"But that responsibility would be mine," she added quickly, interrupting him. "Don't worry, I wouldn't ask for any support, financially or emotionally."

That didn't sit well with Rich, either. He sat back down and leaned forward, pressing his elbows to his knees. He needed to think, but to his dismay he couldn't seem to form a single coherent thought. "Let me see if I understand this correctly," he said after a moment. "You don't want anything from me other than to father your child."

"For this to work, you'd—we'd both need to separate ourselves emotionally from the procedure. The baby would technically be your child, but only because of the genetic makeup. For all intents and purposes, the pregnancy and the child shouldn't be any different than if I'd accepted a donation from the sperm bank."

"In other words all you really want from me is my genes."

"Yes," she said, nodding emphatically. Her gaze briefly met his, and she seemed to have immediate second thoughts. "I know I'm making it all appear so callous, but I don't mean for it to sound that way. There's no one I trust more than you, no one I feel comfortable enough to approach with this idea. If the doctor were to line up ten men... ten strangers and ask me to choose the man who would father my baby, I'd immediately pick you. But knowing you and trusting you means so much more... being we've been friends since high school adds a whole new dimension to this."

"I don't know what to think."

"I ... I considered seducing you."

This time, Rich was unfortunate enough to have a mouthful of coffee he was in the process of swallowing. It stuck halfway down his windpipe and completed its course only after a bout of violent coughing.

"Are you all right?" Jamie asked.

"You honestly considered seducing me?" The idea was even more ludicrous than the first one she'd had.

"Only momentarily," she admitted with some reluctance. "But sex between us would upset everything, don't you think? Your friendship is far too valuable to me to ruin it over something physical."

"I'm pleased to hear it." So she'd honestly considered luring him into her bed. Jamie Warren was certainly full of surprises this evening.

"I'm ... not sure I could have done it," she added as her gaze lowered to her hands, which were tightly clenched in her lap. "I mean ... well, you know what I mean."

Rich wasn't entirely certain he did, but he pretended otherwise by nodding.

Jamie reached for her coffee, took one tentative sip and then stood. "Do you have any questions? I mean, I'm sure you do and I want to reassure you in any way I can."

"Not yet." He couldn't seem to think clearly, let alone form sensible questions. "You say you're not looking for any emotional or financial support?"

"Correct."

"I'm not supposed to feel anything, one way or the other toward this child?"

Her eyes widened briefly. "I ... don't know. I hadn't thought about it in those terms. If it would make it any easier for you, I could move out of the area after the baby's born, or... before. Whichever you prefer."

He didn't like that idea. "What about our parents?"

"What about them?" She seemed puzzled.

Rich couldn't speak for Jamie's mother, but he knew his own, and she'd give him an earful the minute she heard about this craziness. "You don't honestly expect our parents to accept this sitting down, do you?"

"I don't plan to tell them."

The woman was incredible, more so than he'd first assumed. "What do you intend to do? Run off and give birth and then arrive home and present our parents with a surprise grandchild?"

"My mother, yes, but not yours. I don't intend on telling anyone you're the baby's father. That'll be between you and me. No one else need know. As far as my mother's concerned, all she'll know is that I was artificially inseminated, but not by whom. That would only complicate matters, don't you think?"

This didn't sit any better with Rich than some of Jamie's other ideas, especially the one about her moving out of the area. He raked his hand over his face, hoping the action would help him clear his thoughts. It didn't.

"I suppose you'll want a few days to think this over?" She eyed him speculatively. It was apparent she'd like to have her answer as quickly as possible, but that was unfortunate. This was too important a decision to be made quickly. He needed to weigh all the concerns carefully, think through the pros and cons.

Frankly, he found the whole matter unsettling. Sure he'd like to be a father, but personally he'd prefer it to be in the traditional way. His first instinct was to reject her suggestion, but Jamie was staring at him with those big, round eyes of hers, doing her best not to sway him one way or the other. To his regret, Rich found he couldn't reject her suggestion without considering it. Their friendship was worth that much.

"Give me a week," he said after a couple of strained moments.

"A week," she repeated slowly. "Do you want me to call you or will you call me?"

"I'll call you."

She nodded and started to leave, pausing at the front door. "Before I go, there's one thing more I'd like to say."

"Yes."

"I...I honestly believe we would have a beautiful child, but if it isn't meant to be, then I can accept your decision. I'm going to have a child, I'd just rather it was yours than some stranger's." With that, she was out the door.

After she left, unable to stand still, Rich resumed pacing. His thoughts were as tangled as thin gold chains and nearly as impossible to separate. A part of himself was laughing at how absurd Jamie's idea was.

Their baby! Their baby?

They hadn't so much as kissed, and she was proposing they create a child together.

She'd bent over backward to assure him that she expected nothing from him, other than the pregnancy. Although he was certain she hadn't intended the proposition to sound so cold and calculated, that was exactly what Rich was left feeling. She'd made it seem so impersonal. Even that parting shot of hers about them having a beautiful child got to him. With those hazel-green eyes of hers and his height... He forcefully pushed the thought from his head.

Although he'd asked for some time to give the matter consideration, Rich already knew what his answer would be.

He wanted no part of this craziness.

Jamie made an honest effort not to think about Rich for the next few days. She'd made her case, explained what needed to be explained without dressing it up with a long list of emotions or needs.

A hundred or more times since their talk, she'd thought of all the things she might have said to get him to agree to father her child.

Her thoughts were muddled with regrets. Rich was a good friend. Too good to risk ruining their relationship because she was determined to bear a child.

She'd insulted him. She'd known, from his stunned look, his first instinct had been to reject the idea. Good grief, who wouldn't? It was only because they meant so much to each other that he'd been courteous enough to consider her proposal.

Not for the first time, Jamie repressed the urge to contact him and withdraw the suggestion. With everything in her, she wished she hadn't said a word to Rich. And in the same instant she prayed with all her heart, with all her being, he'd be willing to give her a part of himself. She wanted a child, Rich's child, so badly her heart ached every time she thought about what it would mean to them both.

If only she had approached him differently.

If only she had told him how much his child would mean to her, how she'd love the child for a lifetime.

If only she'd assured him what a good mother she intended to be.

If only...

* * *

Rich had made plans with his brother Jason to meet on Sunday afternoon at his apartment and watch the Seahawks football game. Since Rich had given Bill Hastings their fifty-yard-line tickets, the least Rich thought he could do was bring the beer.

Close to one, nearly an hour late, Rich arrived at his brother's with a six-pack of Jason's favorite beer in one hand and a sack full of junk food in the other.

"It's about time you got here," Jason muttered when he opened the front door. "The kick-off's in less than five minutes."

"I brought a peace offering," Rich announced, holding up the six-pack. It wasn't like Rich to be late, and he half expected an interrogation from his brother. He was grateful when it looked as though he was going to escape that. If Jason did grill him, Rich didn't know what he'd say. Certainly not the truth. That he'd been so consumed with indecision over Jamie's proposal, he'd lost track of the time.

"It's going to take a whole lot more than a few beers to make up for the loss of those tickets, little brother," Jason complained, as he led Rich to the sofa. "The last I heard, the scalpers were getting a hundred bucks for this game, and my dear, sweet brother ended up *giving* ours away." There was more than a touch of sarcasm in Jason's droll voice. "I still don't understand what led up to Bill Hastings getting *our* tickets."

Rich had been purposely vague about the exchange. "He did me a favor."

"You couldn't have taken him to dinner?"

"No." It wouldn't help matters any to tell Jason the big favor Bill was supposed to have done him had fallen through. Damn, but that Jamie was a stubborn woman.

She'd do it, too. She'd go ahead and have her baby without him.

The thought stopped him in his tracks. He straightened. That was her decision, naturally. What bothered Rich, what caught him so completely by surprise was the rush of resentment at the thought of her bearing another man's child.

"Hey, you all right?" Jason asked, claiming the seat next to him on the overstuffed sofa.

"Of course I'm all right. Why shouldn't I be?"

"I don't know, but you got this funny look about you as though you swallowed that can of beer whole."

Rich dropped his gaze to the can clenched in his hand, as though he were seeing it for the first time. He offered his brother a weak smile and then relaxed against the cushion. It took a few minutes before his heart rate returned to normal. By George, Jamie would bear a stranger's child. She'd do it in a second. More than once Rich had bumped heads with that stubborn pride of hers, and there wasn't a doubt in his mind.

She'd do it!

"You ever thought much about being a father?" Rich found himself asking his older brother. He attempted to make the question sound casual, but if he succeeded or not was left to be seen.

"Who, me?" Jason teased. "I'm not even married, and frankly I don't ever intend to be."

"Why not?" This was news to Rich. Jason dated nearly as often as Rich did, although he might have led his brother into thinking his social life was more active than it really was. It seemed to him Jason never lacked for gorgeous women. The only time he'd ever gotten serious, the relationship had turned out badly, but that had been years earlier.

"I'm not the marrying kind," Jason announced, tearing open the bag of potato chips with his teeth. "All women think about is reforming me. Hell, if I want to kick off my shoes and watch a football game on a rainy Sunday afternoon, I don't want to feel guilty about it. Most married men are henpecked to death. I prefer my freedom."

"So do I," Rich agreed with a hard shake of his head. Marriage wasn't for him, either. Or Jamie. He appreciated his independence. So did she. Jason apparently felt the same way—women were too damn much trouble.

"If I want to dry my socks in the microwave, there's no one around to be outraged," Jason added, then took a deep swallow of his beer.

"You dried your socks in the microwave?"

The older Manning shrugged. "I forgot to put the load from the washer into the dryer the night before. I needed a pair for work that morning. It was either that or pop them in the toaster."

Rich chuckled. That sounded exactly like something his brother would do. Jason was right about that, too. A woman would have been fit to be tied had she known his preferred method of drying socks.

For the next several minutes they both became engrossed in the game playing on the television. At the commercial break, Jason leaned back and propped up his ankle on his knee.

"What makes you bring up this marriage thing?"

"Nothing much, I was just wondering."

"What about you?" Jason asked, looking to Rich. "Isn't it time you thought about settling down and fathering a houseful of kids?"

"Me?" Rich asked.

"Yes, you. Mom knows any future Mannings are going to have to come from you and Paul. She's thrown her hands up in disgust at me."

"I don't think I'll marry, either."

Jason's eyes widened with disbelief. "Why not?"

"Don't look so surprised."

"I am. You, my dear younger brother, are definitely the marrying kind. Women flock to you in droves."

Plainly his older brother had an elevated view of Rich's sexual prowess, and Rich couldn't see any reason to disillusion him with anything close to the truth. "That's true enough, but not one of them, in all these years, has struck my fancy enough for me to want to marry them."

"What about Pamela?"

"That woman's a . . ." Rich thought better of saying it. "Let's just say we don't have much in common."

"I thought you were still seeing her."

"I do occasionally." He took a swig of his beer and set it down and reached for a bowl of popcorn. Leaning back, he rested his feet on top of the coffee table, crossing his ankles. "This is the life." He made a point of changing the subject, growing uncomfortable with the topic, although he'd been the one foolish enough to introduce it.

"It doesn't get much better than this," Jason returned enthusiastically.

Once again their attention reverted back to the television screen. The Seahawks, the Seattle football team, was playing their archrival, the Denver Broncos, in a heated contest for the American Football Conference Title. The winner would go on to play in the Super Bowl. All of Seattle was hyped up for the game.

"What about kids?" Rich wanted to kick himself the instant the question left his lips. What the hell was the matter with him? He had had no intention of quizzing Jason about any of this when he'd arrived that afternoon.

"Children?" Jason's attention didn't stray from the football game. "What about them?"

"If you don't plan to marry, how do you feel about not having a son?" This plagued Rich the most. He really would like a son. He supposed Jamie would call him a chauvinist. A daughter would be fine, too, but his real heart's desire was for a son.

Jason took a long time answering, as though the question had caught him unprepared. "I don't know...I hadn't given children much thought. I'd like a couple of kids someday, but on the other hand, I don't want to go through the hassle of marrying in order to have them. But then—" he hesitated "—there's no need to marry...not these days. We live in the age of enlightenment, remember?"

"Not marry the woman pregnant with my child?" Rich gave his brother a sour look. "I don't care what age we're living in. We both know better than that. You surprise me, Jason. A word of advice—don't let Mom or Dad ever hear you suggest such a thing."

Jason forcefully exhaled. "You're right, that was a stupid idea." He reached over to the bowl of popcorn Rich was holding and grabbed a handful. "Is there something you're not telling me?"

"Not telling you?" Rich asked.

"Yeah. There's something on your mind."

"I'll tell you what's on my mind," Rich said, reaching for his beer. "Football. That's what's troubling me. In case you haven't noticed, we're down by seven points and Denver's got the ball on the fifteen-yard line." He laughed, but his brother didn't.

"You're sure?" Jason asked a few minutes later.

"Positive," Rich assured him, feigning a smile. A man didn't tell his older brother, especially one who assumed women flocked to him in droves, that he was seriously considering becoming a sperm donor.

Six days had passed, and if Rich didn't contact her soon, Jamie was convinced she was going to suffer a nervous breakdown. Every time the phone rang, her heart zoomed to her throat and she started to tremble like an October leaf.

Rich had made a point of claiming he'd be the one to contact her, and he'd promised to do so within a week's time. Nevertheless, the waiting was killing her. Each day that passed seemed to increase her anxiety a hundredfold.

A casserole was cooking in the oven when the doorbell chimed. Jamie's gaze flew apprehensively toward the front door. Even before she answered it, she knew it was Rich.

Inhaling a steadying breath, she walked across the carpet and opened the door for him.

"Hello, Jamie."

"Rich."

His eyes refused to meet hers, and her stomach twisted into a tight knot as he entered her home. He removed his coat and hung it in the closet as though he intended on staying a long while. Jamie didn't know whether she should take encouragement from that or not.

"I just put dinner in the oven. Will you join me?"

He nodded, although she was convinced he hadn't heard what she'd said.

"It's a new recipe.... I seem to be in a cooking mode lately. Tamale pie—I found the recipe on the back of a package of cornmeal. I've always enjoyed Mexican food."

"Me, too."

"Would you care for some coffee?"

"Sure."

He followed her into the kitchen and sat down at the table. "I suppose you're wondering what I've decided," he said when she delivered his coffee to him.

It demanded every ounce of fortitude she possessed not to demand he tell her then and there. Waiting even a minute more seemed too long. She pulled out the chair across from him and sat down. She was so anxious, her hands were trembling and she clenched them together in her lap, not wanting to give herself away.

"I've done a good deal of thinking in the past several days," he said bluntly.

If the lines about his eyes and mouth were any indication, his thoughts had been deep and probing. It didn't look as though he'd slept much in the last week. For that matter neither had she.

"I'm sure it hasn't been an easy decision."

"You're damn right it hasn't," he said pointedly. "Before I say anything more, there are a few things I want to get straight. Once I do, you may change your mind yourself."

"I'm not going to do that," Jamie said with supreme confidence.

His piercing eyes held hers. "Don't be so sure. First and foremost, I want full parental privileges. This child will be as much a part of me as he or she is of you." He spoke forcefully, as though he anticipated an argument from her.

"What...what exactly do you mean by parental privileges?"

"I want a say in how the child will be raised, as much a say as you. This means that when it comes time to choosing a preschool, I'll expect you to confer with me. I don't want you moving out of the area, either—that should be clear right now. At least not without me being informed and in full agreement, but I can tell you right now, I won't agree."

"All right," she agreed hesitantly. The only reason she'd even brought up the subject of moving was to make matters simpler for him. It wasn't what she wanted or what she intended. "Anything else?"

"I'm just getting started. If we go ahead with this, I want visitation rights."

"Of course. I have no intention of hiding the child from you."

"That's not what I understood earlier." He frowned, as if rankled.

"I...know. I should have thought matters through more carefully before I approached you. I'd come up with the idea of you being the baby's father the same night as I asked you. When I arrived at your place, the idea was only half formed."

Rich seemed cold and distant, as though they were discussing highly sensitive political material and there was no room for friendliness. No room for personal feelings.

"Does this mean you've changed your mind?" he demanded.

"No...no, just that I hadn't thought everything through as extensively as I should have before I came to you. It hadn't dawned on me that you'd care one way or the other toward the child... I realize now how insensitive that was of me. I apologize for that, Rich, I really do feel bad about my attitude."

"Of course I'd care about the child."

"I realize that now. If you want full visitation rights, and a say in how the child is brought up, then that's only fair. I have no objections. None whatsoever."

"I'm also going to insist you accept child support."

"But, Rich, that really isn't necessary. I make a decent wage and..." She stopped abruptly at the way his eyes hardened. They resembled blue chips of ice.

"Then the whole deal's off."

She took a moment to compose herself. "Since that's clearly an important issue with you, then naturally I'll be more than willing to accept whatever monetary support you deem necessary."

"Emotional support, as well. I don't want you walking the floors at night with a colicky baby."

"What do you expect me to do?"

"Phone me."

He was making everything seem so much more complicated than it needed to be. "You don't honestly expect me to call you over every little thing do you?"

"Yes," he stated emphatically. "I want everything as clear as glass between us before the blessed event. The child will be a part of me as much as he is of you. We'll share the responsibility and the duties."

"He?"

"Or she. But if I'm given the option, then I'd prefer a son."

"Naturally. But let it be known, I'd prefer a daughter, so let's just leave that decision with Mother Nature."

"Having second thoughts yet?" Rich wanted to know.

"Not . . . really. If you're sure this is everything."

"It isn't." He stood and opened the oven door, checking the casserole that was baking inside. He let it close slowly.

"You mean there's more?"

"One small item."

"One small item," Jamie repeated, confident she wouldn't have any more trouble with this than his other points.

"If we do decide to go ahead and have a child together . . ."

"And I think we should," she said, smiling over at him.

"Fine. Great. Wonderful. If you're sure."

"I'm sure."

"Good. In that case, I insist we marry."

Chapter Four

Jamie was too confused to think clearly. Surely Rich didn't mean what he'd said. It made no sense. "Marry . . . but . . . you can't be serious."

"I've rarely been more serious in my life," Rich answered, stalking to the far side of her kitchen. He removed two dinner plates from her cupboard and set them on the table. "Naturally, this wouldn't be a conventional marriage."

"Naturally," Jamie echoed, still too bewildered to interpret his reasoning. "Then . . . why are you insisting we go through with a wedding?"

"I want the child to have my name."

"Oh."

"We'll continue to maintain our separate residences. For all intents and purposes, nothing will change, at least not outwardly."

Jamie stood in front of the silverware drawer and closed her eyes, trying to force her heart to quit pounding so fast and hard. Rich had made it plain this wasn't any love match—not that she'd suspected it ever would be. Nevertheless, her heart had reacted fiercely to the suggestion.

"What about the pregnancy? I mean ... how do you intend for me to become pregnant?" By the time the question was complete, her voice had dwindled to a whisper.

"You could always seduce me."

Furious, Jamie whirled around and glared heatedly at Rich. She could feel the color warming her cheeks, creeping up her neckline like blood filling a sponge. "I should never have admitted that. You're going to throw it in my face at every opportunity, aren't you?"

"No," he denied, but his eyes were sparkling with the blue light of laughter. "I agree with you. Sex between us would ruin everything. I don't want to risk our friendship any more than you do."

The tension eased from between Jamie's shoulder blades.

"We'll need to keep the marriage a secret."

"For how long?" If their child was to have his name, they'd eventually be forced into making an explanation. Jamie wasn't keen on facing her mother with a surprise marriage to go along with a pregnancy. Doris Warren wouldn't take kindly to being cheated out of a wedding any more than his own mother would.

"We'd only stay married until the baby's born," Rich explained, revealing no hint of indecision, and certainly no doubts. He apparently had everything worked out in his mind, neatly tied up in a bright bow.

Unfortunately, he'd completely unsettled Jamie. She'd had everything organized in her own mind and none of what she intended included marriage, even one of convenience. The questions were popping up faster than popcorn kernels sizzling in hot grease.

"What are we going to say after the baby's born?" she demanded.

"That we're getting a divorce."

Jamie felt the sudden need to sit back down. "That we're divorcing?" she repeated slowly. Already she could imagine her mother's shock and dismay. Not only had Jamie married without telling her, but she was about to obtain a divorce.

"It makes sense once you think about it," Rich continued with matchless confidence.

Maybe it did to him, but Jamie felt as though she were wandering through the dark, lost and confused, bumping into walls she didn't know were there. It had all seemed so simple the night she'd approached Rich.

He pulled out the chair and lifted his foot onto the seat. He leaned toward her, bracing his elbow across his knee. "We'll get married at the courthouse, as quietly as possible. There isn't any reason for anyone to know."

"That much I understand.... I'm just not convinced it's necessary."

"I am," he said adamantly.

"All right, all right," she said, holding back the hair from her forehead while she attempted to think clearly. What had seemed such an uncomplicated idea had suddenly taken on more twists and turns than a California turnpike.

"You'll agree to the wedding?"

"I don't know yet."

"Don't sound so enthusiastic."

"I'm not," she muttered.

"As soon as the ink's dry on the marriage certificate we can make an appointment with the gynecologist...."

"Good grief, what are we going to tell him?" Jamie didn't relish that task. If Rich wanted to explain why two healthy, normal married adults would choose such an unconventional method to get her pregnant, then more power to him. Frankly, she was staying away from this one.

"We won't tell him anything. He's a professional—he isn't going to ask a lot of questions."

"Rich...I don't know about this."

"If you have any doubts, then I suggest you air them now."

"I'm not sure we're doing the right thing. We don't have to go through a wedding ceremony for the baby to have your name. Couldn't you legally adopt her after she's born?"

"Why complicate everything?"

"And marriage isn't going to do that?" Jamie cried.

"Marriage will accomplish the same thing now without the legal hassles of adoption later. As I explained earlier, it'll be in name only."

"Yes, I know, but..." She hesitated and took a few moments to shape her objections in the form of a reasonable argument. When she spoke, her eyes met his. "You're going to think I'm terribly old-fashioned."

"The woman who asked me to be the sperm donor for her child? Never!"

Jamie had the feeling it would take a good long while for her to live that down. "Yes," she said vehemently, "I suppose it has to do with my upbringing, but I've always considered marriage sacred. It's nothing to take lightly. Somehow, it just doesn't feel right to be quietly married and...and then arrange for a divorce nine months later.''

Rich went quiet for several moments. ''I agree, but this isn't a normal marriage.''

''What marriage is?'' Jamie asked, thinking of all the friends she'd known over the years who'd married. Each and every relationship was different from the others. She'd silently stood by and observed how some couples had grown closer and stronger in their love and commitment to one another. Other married couples had drifted further and further apart until it was all she could do not to plead with them to do something before it was too late.

''Nothing's going to change, at least not outwardly,'' Rich tried to reassure her once again. ''We're doing this for the sake of the child and for you.''

''For me?'' Jamie wasn't sure she understood.

Rich's eyes narrowed slightly, and when he spoke his voice was as cold and hard as steel. ''I won't allow your reputation to be marred by this pregnancy.''

That was all well and good, but it was her reputation and if she had no objections, then he need not be concerned. ''But, Rich—''

''And furthermore,'' he said heatedly, interrupting her. ''I refuse to allow my son or daughter to be born a bastard.''

Any argument Jamie could have raised was erased with this one, simple statement. ''You've got a point,'' she whispered.

''I can understand your hesitation.''

Jamie lowered her gaze. ''It's just that I fully expect you will marry someday. Sooner or later a woman's going to come into your life and this marriage is going to complicate everything for you. What are you going to tell 'her' about me . . . and the child?''

"The truth."

"But, Rich—"

"It's not going to happen. If I believed I was eventually going to marry, I wouldn't have agreed to this."

He sounded so sincere that any doubts Jamie entertained were wiped out with the richness of his smile.

"So you'll marry me?"

Jamie nodded. She wasn't convinced it was the right thing for them to do, but it was necessary.

"There's one last thing," Rich said, lowering his foot to the floor and wrapping his hands around the back of her kitchen chair.

There was more? Jamie's head was still reeling from his last announcement. "Now what?"

"You're important to me. Our friendship is important. For the sake of our relationship, I think we should have everything drawn up legally. I don't want there to be any misunderstandings later."

This made a good deal of sense to Jamie. "I agree, but ninety per cent of the lawyers I know would laugh us out of their offices. This isn't the usual contract, you know."

"There's one I know who'll do it. One I trust."

"Who?"

"James Wilkens, the man Christy was engaged to marry."

James Wilkens's office reminded Rich of his youngest sister, Christy. He'd stopped in a couple of times over the past year to take his sister to lunch, and he half expected her to come around the corner at any moment.

Christy was married to Cody, however, not James. Sheriff Cody Franklin. Rich wasn't likely to forget how he'd interrupted their wedding night, nor was Cody going to let him forget it. Rich had arrived at her apartment soon after he'd found out about Pamela's little fling. He'd been disgusted and disheartened, convinced women didn't know the meaning of the word *faithful*. His thinking hadn't included Christy, though. Not his little sister; she had always been so sweet and virtuous. Then, not knowing they were married, he'd stumbled upon her in bed with Cody, and his opinion of women had dipped to an all-time low.

Sitting in the plushly decorated waiting room next to a five-foot potted philodendron brought back an abundance of memories. The plant was on one side and a fidgeting Jamie on the other.

His gaze lazily wandered to Jamie, who was flipping through the pages of a magazine fast enough to create a draft. She was on her third issue of *Good Housekeeping* and they hadn't been seated for more than five minutes.

She remained diffident to the idea of this marriage, but she wanted the child enough to agree to his terms.

Unlike Jamie, Rich felt comfortable with the plan, for all the reasons he'd given her. He wasn't sure how anyone else would think, especially his family, but frankly that was their problem. He was marrying his best friend, and a whole lot could be said for marriage between friends.

Rich had the almost overwhelming urge to laugh. Never, even in his wildest imagination had he ever thought he'd agree to anything like this. According to Jason, women naturally gravitated toward him. In some ways that was true, but generally, they were the wrong kind of women. What he wouldn't give to have found a woman as genuine and as compassionate as Jamie.

The need to touch her, to reassure her even in the smallest of ways was as strong as the urge to laugh had been a few minutes earlier. He reached for her hand, entwining her fingers with his own.

She glanced up at him. "I'm sorry."

"For what?"

"I . . . I can't seem to sit still."

"We aren't at the courthouse, you know. This is a meeting with James. He's a decent guy, and a damn good attorney. He isn't going to laugh or make snide remarks."

"I know. . . . It's just that . . ." She let the rest of the sentence fade.

"You're nervous."

"I'm nervous," she agreed with one abrupt nod. "I don't understand why exactly, but my stomach's in knots and I can't seem to read, and I keep thinking of all the things that could go wrong."

"Like what?"

Jamie turned from him and lowered her gaze to the open magazine in her lap. "I . . . you wouldn't understand."

"Try me."

"Marriage isn't something to be taken lightly. I know I've said that before, but I can't seem to explain it in a way that'll make you understand the seriousness of this. Something happens to a couple when they marry . . . even when it's only a marriage of convenience. Something spiritual. I know you don't agree with me, but we're both going to be affected by this. I can't shake the feeling that deep down we're going to regret this someday."

"We aren't going to share a physical relationship."

"I know all that," she argued, "but it doesn't change what I feel."

Her hand was trembling in his, and he knew from the way her voice dipped and rose that she was close to tears. "Do you want to call the whole thing off?" Rich would bow to Jamie's wishes, but he sincerely hoped she wouldn't back down now.

"That's the crazy part," she said, looking even more tense than before. "I want this marriage and our child more than I've wanted anything in my life."

"So do I," Rich admitted, realizing how true it was. "So do I."

"Rich," James greeted, sauntering into the waiting room. Rich stood and the two exchanged hearty handshakes. "It was a pleasant surprise to find your name on my appointment calendar this morning." The attorney's gaze drifted from Rich to Jamie, and he smiled warmly.

"This is Jamie Warren," Rich explained.

"Hello."

"We met briefly...a little while back," she said, suddenly biting off her words. She cast an embarrassed, regretful look toward Rich as though she'd made a dreadful blunder. It wasn't until they were inside James's office that Rich remembered the two had been introduced at James and Christy's engagement party.

"Come on in and sit down," James said, motioning toward the two upholstered chairs that were positioned on the other side of his desk. James was of medium height with broad shoulders and a hairline that was just beginning to recede.

Rich knew from mutual acquaintances that James had taken the broken engagement with Christy hard.

He'd loved Rich's youngest sister and had been deeply wounded when she'd married Cody. Rich had heard James rarely dated. If it was true, that was a shame. James had a lot to offer a woman. He was a junior partner with the firm these days and his talents were in high demand. It would take one hell of a woman to replace Christy, and Rich sincerely hoped James would take the time to find her.

"So," James said, reaching for his pen and a yellow pad, "what can I do for you?"

Rich leaned against the back of the chair and relaxed. "Jamie and I would like for you to draw us up a prenuptial agreement."

The attorney's gaze flew to Rich's. "Congratulations. I couldn't be more pleased. I hadn't heard you were engaged."

"We aren't...exactly," Jamie explained hurriedly. When James focused his attention on her, she shifted her weight in the chair and motioned to Rich. "You'd better explain...everything."

"This will be a marriage of convenience."

"A marriage of convenience," James repeated slowly, as though he wasn't entirely certain he'd understood Rich correctly.

"There are extenuating circumstances."

"We're going to have a baby," Jamie inserted, then as she realized what she'd implied, her eyes grew wide with concern. "I'm not pregnant, at least not yet, but if everything goes according to schedule, I will be within the next couple of months."

James leaned against the back of his chair and held on to the two ends of his pen. "This doesn't sound like a marriage of convenience to me."

"We aren't going to destroy a perfectly wonderful friendship with sex," Jamie declared vehemently, slicing the air with her hands. "We agreed on that, first thing."

The pen was carefully placed on top of the polished mahogany desk. James's gaze was leveled on Rich as though he were having a difficult time reserving his opinion. "Let me see if I understand this correctly. You intend for Jamie to become pregnant, but there isn't going to be any sex?"

"Before we go any further, I want the details of the divorce clearly spelled out," Jamie added, scooting to the edge of her cushioned seat and sitting on her hands. She continued to fidget the same way she had in the waiting room, crossing and uncrossing her ankles. "They should be as explicitly drawn up as the particulars of the marriage. And by the way, we won't be living together. But that shouldn't matter, should it?"

"You're planning the divorce now?" This time, James made a few notations on the pad. He scratched the side of his head and frowned anew.

"You don't honestly expect us to stay married after the baby's born, do you?"

"Rich?" James looked to him, his brow continuing to compress. "Would you kindly explain what's going on here?"

"We're getting married, having a baby and getting a divorce. A, B, C. Points one, two and three. It's not nearly as complicated as it sounds." Rich found he was enjoying this. James, however, clearly wasn't.

"A prenuptial agreement I understand. We have several forms drawn up that you can read over. The two of you can decide which one suits you best."

"But what about the baby and the divorce?" Jamie asked nervously, then looking to Rich, added, "I don't think James understands what we're planning."

"You're right about that. The marriage I understand—at least I think I do. Unfortunately it's everything else that's got me confused."

"There's a logical explanation for all this," Rich eloquently assured him.

"No, there isn't," Jamie countered sharply. "Rich insists we marry and I honestly don't feel it's necessary, but nothing I can say will convince him otherwise. If I didn't want a baby so much, I'd never agree to this."

"Rich?" Once again, James looked to him. It was apparent he was more baffled than ever. His gaze continued to move from Jamie to Rich and then back again.

"It's not as confusing as it sounds," Rich assured him one more time. "A bit complicated and unconventional, but not confusing." He spent the next ten minutes explaining their plans and answering a long series of pointed questions from the attorney.

"It sounds crazy, doesn't it?" Jamie asked once Rich had finished. "You probably think we both need to make an appointment at a mental-health clinic. I don't blame you, I really don't."

James took his own sweet time answering, Rich noted. He continued making notes, then raised his head to look pointedly at Rich. "Are you sure this is what you want?"

"I'm sure." Rich shared few of Jamie's concerns regarding the marriage. It was merely a formality. She kept talking about it as though it were a deep spiritual experience. For some couples, marriage might well be that. But not for Jamie and him.

"What about you, Jamie?"

Her head came up sharply.

"Are you sure this is what you want?" James repeated the question slowly.

She hesitated, then shook her head emphatically. "I'm sure."

James paused and rolled the pen between his open palms as though collecting his thoughts. "Does your family know anything about your plans?" The question was directed at Rich.

He gave a short, scoffing laugh. "You've got to be joking. I don't intend for them to find out, either. At least not right away. They'll learn about the marriage and the baby eventually—that much is inevitable. But the longer I can keep this from my parents, the better."

"On that much, I can agree."

"You'll write up an agreement for us?" Rich asked. He didn't miss the subtle note of concern in James's well-modulated voice.

"I'll have one drawn up within a week."

"Good." Rich reached for Jamie's hand. They both stood, and she tucked the long strap of her purse over her shoulder. "Then we'll go off to the courthouse and apply for the wedding license."

"Might I offer you two a bit of advice?" James asked, standing himself. He rubbed the side of his jaw as if he wasn't quite sure, even now, what he wanted to say.

"Please." Jamie sounded as though she were looking for someone to talk her out of this scheme. If that was the case, Rich would be the first one to remind her that the entire idea had been hers.

"I'll write up whatever it is you want me to," James said slowly, thoughtfully, "but I don't believe there's any reason to rush into this. You've both waited this long to start a family—a few more months one way or the other isn't going to change anything.''

Rich looked to Jamie for confirmation, but he couldn't read her thoughts. ''We'll talk about it,'' Rich promised.

James nodded. ''I'll give you a call later in the week and you can stop off and read over the agreement.''

''Great.'' Rich steered Jamie toward the door, although she didn't need any encouragement. She seemed downright eager to escape. ''I'll be talking to you soon then,'' Rich said over his shoulder.

''Soon,'' James promised.

Jamie was quiet on her way to the parking lot. For that matter so was he. Although James hadn't come right out and expressed his apprehensions, they were there bold as could be. From the questions he'd asked, to the hesitation Rich heard in his voice. Hell, Rich didn't blame him.

Rich unlocked the passenger door and held it open for Jamie. He waited until she was inside, his hand on the door. ''Do you want to take some time to think this over?''

''No,'' she returned automatically. ''Do you?''

He shook his head. ''No.''

Their eyes met and held until they both were smiling broadly.

Rich woke early Tuesday morning, before the alarm sounded. He turned on the shower and stepped under the plummeting spray, enjoying the feel of it against his skin. He was soaping down his torso and whistling when the cheery tune slowly faded out one note at a time.

He quickly finished showering, reached for a thick towel and headed directly from the bathroom to the phone at his bedside. He punched out the number from memory and impatiently waited three long rings before Jamie answered.

"Good morning," he greeted enthusiastically.

"Good morning," came her groggy reply.

"You know what today is, don't you?"

"I'm not likely to forget. It isn't every day a woman gets married."

"Second thoughts?"

"Third and fourth if you want the truth, but now that I've had several days to think everything over, I'm more confident than ever."

"Good." He'd grown anxious in the shower, convinced Jamie would change her mind at the last minute. He had to be assured one last time, although they'd talked of little else in the past week.

James had contacted him Friday afternoon, and Rich had stopped off at the attorney's office on his way home from work. The agreement was several pages thick, but when he asked for the bill, James had insisted it was a wedding present. The gesture took Rich by surprise. James was the only person who knew what they intended, and he was acting as though this was a conventional marriage. Of all people, James was well aware of exactly how unconventional they intended it to be.

"You think we're nuts, don't you?"

"No," James responded with a wry grin. "I think you're both in love and just don't know it yet."

James's claim had caught Rich off guard. He would never have taken the attorney for a romantic.

I think you're both in love and just don't know it yet. On this, the morning of his wedding, Rich tested

James's theory once again. Sure he loved her, but not in the sense James implied. They were friends. Good buds. Not lovers. Not soulmates. Just friends.

"Have you arranged for a witness?" Jamie asked, pulling Rich out of his reverie.

"A witness?"

"Rich—" she groaned "—don't you remember? When we applied for the license, we were told we'd each need to bring along a witness. What do you intend to do, drag someone in from outside the judge's quarters?"

Rich thought about it for a moment. "I suppose so."

"Don't forget the ring," she said, beginning to sound nervous.

"I won't."

"As soon as the ceremony's over, I'll return it." Rich intended to use a small diamond that had once belonged to his grandmother. Jamie had objected, until she'd come upon the idea of returning it after the ceremony. A diamond would raise too many questions, she'd decided. The only reason they even needed one was for the exchange of vows.

"Who's going to be your witness?"

Jamie paused. She couldn't very well ask any of her friends. "I...I'm not sure yet. I was thinking of Marge from New Accounts. Marge can keep a secret, but then I thought it might not be a good idea if anyone from the bank knew I was getting married."

"What do you intend to do?" he asked, mimicking her words. "Drag someone in from outside the judge's quarters?"

"I suppose so," she returned, and laughed. It had been a week or longer since Rich had heard the sound of her amusement. It encouraged him, and he chuckled himself.

"You haven't heard from anyone?"

"No. You?"

Their biggest concern was that one or more of their family members would come across their application for a wedding license. Such information was regularly published in the Seattle newspapers. But they hadn't been given any choice in the matter. Anyone who applied for a marriage license had their name published.

In his worst nightmare Rich could envision his mother sobbing hysterically, interrupting the wedding ceremony. No doubt she'd be furious that he was marrying Jamie without the large church ceremony she'd always looked forward to holding for Taylor and Christy. Both of Rich's sisters had opted for a small private wedding without any family present. And he was doing the same thing.

The family honor now rested in Jason's hands.

Jason.

"Rich." Jamie's voice cut into his thoughts. "Don't worry, I'll have a witness."

Rich paused a few moments later, his fingers poised at the stiff fasteners of his white shirt. He finished dressing, in a hurry now, his movements filled with purpose.

He grabbed his raincoat on his way out the door and found himself whistling once more as he unlocked his car. He checked his watch, and realized he had plenty of time. More time than he knew what to do with.

He drove to his brother's veterinary hospital in the south end of Seattle. There he found three people in the waiting room. Two in the section marked Dogs and one little old lady clinging tightly to her cat on the other side of the room.

"Is Jason in?" he asked the receptionist.

"He's with a Saint Bernard, but he'll be out in a few minutes."

Sure enough, Jason appeared no more than five minutes later. He wore a white coat, but underneath, Rich knew he had on jeans and a T-shirt.

"Rich, what are you doing here?"

"Can you take off for an hour later on today?"

"You taking me to lunch?" Jason asked.

"No, I need you to stand up as my best man for my wedding."

Chapter Five

Jamie was at the courthouse at the agreed time, pacing the corridor outside Judge Webster's chambers.

She was there, but Rich wasn't.

If he left her standing at the altar, she'd personally see to his tar and feathering.

For the tenth time in the past minute, she checked her watch.

Seven minutes late. The man would pay for this.

A woman Jamie assumed was the judge's secretary stepped into the hallway. "The judge can see you now."

"Ah . . . hello," Jamie said, giving the middle-aged woman her brightest smile. "My . . . the man I'm going to marry seems to have been detained. I'm sure he'll be here any second."

"I see." She checked her watch as though to say the judge was a busy man.

"I'm sure he'll be here." She was of the opinion that a slow death would be too good for Rich if he wasn't. "I was wondering...when Rich does arrive, would it be possible for you to be my witness?" She shouldn't have left it for the last minute like this, but she wasn't sure who to ask.

"Of course." The gray-haired woman returned Jamie's smile. "Let me know as soon as your young man arrives."

"I will, thank you."

Jamie resumed her pacing. She'd made the mistake of asking for the day off from work. If she'd only taken half a day, she wouldn't be left with all this time to contemplate what she was doing. In the last five minutes she'd vacillated back and forth any number of times. Apparently Rich had experienced a change of heart himself.

Marrying was the best way. It was right for them, right for their baby.

It was the most foolish decision she'd ever made.

"Jamie." Breathless, Rich came around the corner in a half run.

"Where have you been?" she cried, her voice cracking under the strain. She was caught halfway between abject relief and frustrated fury. Halfway between hope and despair, trapped in a world of nagging questions and second thoughts.

Rich pulled her into his arms and hugged her close. His breathing was labored, as though he'd raced up several flights of stairs. "I got held up in traffic."

Jamie was about to chastise him for not allowing enough time, but she swallowed her irritation. What did it matter? He was there now, and she experienced a relief so great it was all she could do not to wrap her arms around him and weep.

"Judge Webster's secretary said we should go into his office once you arrive," she said, composing herself.

"Just a minute. We need to wait for my witness," Rich said, and smiled down at her. His beautiful blue gaze filled with a teasing light.

"You actually brought someone with you? Who?"

"Me," Jason Manning said, hurrying around the same corner Rich had seconds earlier. He, too, appeared out of breath. "Rich left me to park the car," he said, pressing his hand over his heart. "Said if he was late for this wedding you'd skin him alive."

"He was right, too."

Jamie's gaze flew to Rich, whose expression was both tender and amused. He'd brought family! They'd discussed the subject at length and had agreed not to let any of their immediate relations in on their plans. Not until it was necessary, which they'd roughly calculated was when Jamie entered the fifth or sixth month of her pregnancy.

"Bringing Jason seemed like a good idea at the time," Rich explained, wearing a chagrined look. "He spent half the morning arguing with me. According to Jason, we're candidates for the loony bin."

"We weren't going to tell anyone, remember?" With damn good reason. The fewer people who were in on this, the better. The route they'd chosen to produce an offspring was sure to raise more than a few eyebrows. At the rate Rich was telling people, Jamie wouldn't be surprised to see her picture splashed across the front of a grocery store tabloid.

"Don't worry," Jason inserted smoothly, "I've been sworn to secrecy."

"I'll explain everything later," Rich promised under his breath. He draped his arm over her shoulder and exhaled sharply as though he still needed to catch his breath. "But for right now, we've got a wedding to see to."

Jamie realized the ceremony itself wouldn't last more than a few minutes. She'd taken comfort in knowing that. They'd be in and out of the judge's chambers in five minutes, ten tops.

They stood before Judge Webster their backs stiff and at attention. The judge attempted to reassure them with a smile.

Jamie needed to be reassured. Her knees were shaking, her hands trembled and she wasn't sure she was going to be able to go through with this.

When it came time for her to repeat her vows, she hesitated and lifted her eyes to Rich. How could she promise to love him, honor him throughout the rest of their lives, knowing full well their marriage wouldn't last out the year?

Rich must have read her confusion and her doubt. Some unfathomable emotion flickered in his eyes, and she wondered if he, too, were experiencing the same doubts. His hold on her hand tightened slightly, lending her his strength. Jamie felt the need to be close to him. She didn't analyze the why of it any more than she could evaluate the reason she'd agreed to go through with the wedding ceremony.

When she spoke, her voice fluttered like an aspen leaf, then leveled and grew steady and strong. Her heart was pounding fast and furious, then gradually returned to a normal, even beat. She realized that the calmness that had come over her, the serenity, had come from Rich. His gaze didn't leave hers, and when he spoke, his own voice was confident and sure.

They exchanged rings, his hand holding hers as he slipped onto her finger the delicate diamond that had belonged to his grandmother. His grasp was solid, and he revealed no hesitation. Once the ring was secure, her gaze slowly traveled the distance upward to his face. She stopped at his eyes, so blue and clear. They were just as steady as his hand.

The judge pronounced them man and wife, and with a naturalness Jamie didn't question, Rich drew her into his embrace. Her hands gripped hold of his shoulders as he slowly lowered his mouth to hers. To the best of Jamie's memory, this was the first time they'd kissed, really kissed.

Rich made it worth the wait.

His mouth slid possessively over hers, coaxing open her lips. His own were warm and moist, gentle and teasing, giving and demanding.

Jamie couldn't credit the wide variety of sensations that swamped her senses. She felt light-headed and giddy. Appreciated and adored. It was as though her entire world had been inadvertently tossed upside down and she was left, groping, to find her balance.

She shouldn't feel this way, she told herself. She shouldn't be experiencing any of these sensations. Rich didn't love her...not like this. Nothing like this. One kiss and he made her feel as though she'd never been kissed before, as though she'd never experienced love before.

Maybe she hadn't. Perhaps this was all part of her imagination, her mind creating a warm romantic fantasy in order to appease her conscience. Maybe this was a subconscious effort to wipe out the ambivalent feelings she'd experienced during the ceremony.

The sound of Rich's older brother clearing his throat brought Jamie back to reality. Rich reluctantly released her and just as reluctantly turned his attention to Judge Webster. The two men exchanged handshakes.

"Thank you so much for being my witness," Jamie said to Judge Webster's secretary. She never did catch the woman's name.

"I was more than pleased to do it," the secretary with the short gray hair returned. She stepped forward and gave Jamie an impulsive hug. "The judge marries several couples every year, you realize, but I have a good feeling about you and your young man. I think you two are going to be just fine. I really do."

Jamie didn't know what to think. She felt like the biggest phony who'd ever lived. Already it was happening. The very thing she had tried to warn Rich about, the feeling of connection. The spiritual linking. She's sensed it during the ceremony and even more so with his kiss.

They were making a mockery of everything a marriage was supposed to be. Jamie had never felt more like weeping in her life.

She'd tried to make light of it. Tried to convince herself they were doing the right thing. Rich was so confident, so sure, and she believed him because . . . because she'd always believed him.

But if they were doing what was right, then why was her stomach in knots? Why did she feel as though she was going to burst into tears? And why, oh why, had Rich kissed her as though she were the most cherished wife in the world?

"Congratulations," Jason said, moving toward her.

She tried to smile, honestly smile, but her mouth started quivering and the tears fell a natural path from the corners of her eyes, running down the sides of her face.

"Jamie?" Jason asked, giving her a hug. "Are you all right?"

"No."

Jamie didn't know how Jason managed it, but within a matter of minutes they were out of Judge Webster's chambers and Rich was at her side, his arm wrapped around her middle.

"All right," he said gently, guiding her down the hallway, "what are the tears all about?"

Jamie rubbed the palm of her hand across her cheeks, convinced she'd smeared mascara over her face in the process. She'd dressed so carefully, opting for a pale pink tailored suit. Like a romantic fool, she'd had her hair styled and nails polished—and for what? So she could stand before God and man and say vows they'd never be able to keep.

"You honestly want to know what's wrong?" she wailed, snapping open her purse and rummaging around for a tissue. She found one, tucked her handbag under her arm and noisily blew her nose. "You mean you don't know?"

"No."

"I . . . I feel dreadful."

"Why?" Rich looked completely stumped.

"Because I just lied."

"Lied?"

"So did you!"

"Me?" Rich sounded all the more confused.

"How can you justify what we just did? We stood before Judge Webster and spoke vows. Vows! Vows are

serious stuff. We made promises to one another, promises neither one of us intend to keep.''

''I can't speak for you, but I certainly intend to honor
my vows.''

''Oh, right,'' Jamie muttered sarcastically, rubbing
the top of her hand beneath her nose. ''You're going to
love me in...in sickness and health and everything else
you said.''

''Yes.'' Rich didn't so much as blink.

''How...can you?''

''True, this might not be a traditional marriage.
Nevertheless, it is a marriage. And I fully intend to
honor every promise I made for the full duration of the
marriage.''

''You do?'' she asked on the tail end of a sniffle.

''You mean you don't?''

''I...I suppose so. It's just that I hadn't thought
about it like that. I do love you, you know...like a
friend.''

''The problem, I think,'' Rich said, walking with her
toward the elevator. His hands were gripped behind his
back as though he were deep in thought. Ever diplo-
matic, Jason remained a few steps behind them. ''The
problem,'' he repeated, ''is that we've both put several
years of effort into finding the perfect mate. We've each
looked so hard for that special person—someone we'd
be comfortable committing the rest of our lives to loving. Neither of us has found what we've been looking
for, so when we stood before Judge Webster...'' He
hesitated as though he'd lost his train of thought.

''What we were pledging...the seriousness of our
decision hit hard,'' Jamie finished for him.

''Exactly,'' Rich agreed, nodding.

"Then you felt it, too?" She stopped walking and turned to face him, her heart in her throat. Her pulse had been increasing in rhythm with each word he spoke. Rich had experienced the same phenomenon that had come over her while they were repeating their vows, too. He'd felt the solemnness of it all the same way she had.

"I did...very much," he whispered. "A wedding ceremony is a sobering affair. If you didn't understand it before, I want it clear now. I'm committed to you, Jamie. That commitment will be the same for the baby once he's born."

"She," Jamie corrected, gnawing on her lower lip. Rich had said as much before in other ways, only she hadn't understood it. He'd insisted upon supplying financial support for their child and emotional support for her. He'd also been the one who'd insisted they marry so the child would bear his name. But she hadn't thought of it as a commitment until he'd mentioned it. She experienced relief, and contentment stole through her.

They continued walking, side by side, toward the elevator, which was at the far end of the marble corridor. Rich matched his stride to hers. He was several inches taller than Jamie, head and shoulders taller. Every once in a while his shoulder would brush against her. His touch felt intimate and special. Jamie was sure he didn't mean for her to experience anything at his touch, but she did. She couldn't help herself.

"It's going to be all right, isn't it?" she asked when they stopped to wait for the elevator.

"Not if our parents find out about this, it won't be," Jason answered for Rich.

"They won't anytime soon unless you tell them." A clear warning was woven in with Rich's words.

"Hey," Jason said, raising his right hand. "I've already promised not to say a word...to anyone. Mom and Dad would have to torture it out of me."

Rich chuckled and slowly shook his head. "All Mom would ever need to do was offer you homemade bread fresh from the oven."

"Maybe so. But be warned, the fur's going to fly once she learns she missed out on the wedding of another one of her children."

"She'll adjust," Rich argued, looping his arm over Jamie's shoulder.

"Are you as full as I am?" Rich asked, leaning back against the thick cushion of the circular booth. His hands rested over his flat stomach and he breathed in deeply.

"I couldn't eat another bite if I tried." Rich had made reservations for their wedding dinner at the restaurant at the top of the world-famous Space Needle. He'd planned every aspect of their wedding day celebration, from the matinee tickets he'd purchased for a musical playing at the Fifth Avenue Theater, to a special dinner.

"I still don't understand what Jason meant when he claimed you kidnapped him?" she asked, basking in the richness of the most memorable day of her life.

Rich reached for the wine bottle and replenished both their glasses. "To be honest, I did kidnap him. Why...is another story. I'm not sure myself, especially when I knew he'd try to talk me out of this."

"He did try, didn't he?" That much went without saying.

"Not at first." Rich arched a brow as though he remained a bit surprised at that. "He seemed downright excited until he heard the full details."

Jamie groaned. "You told him...everything?"

"He's my brother." Rich reached for his wineglass and sipped from the edge of the crystal. "When I first told him about you and me, he couldn't have been more pleased. He said he's always admired you and felt I couldn't have made a better choice."

"He said that?" Jamie couldn't help feeling a little incredulous. She barely knew Rich's older brother. Oh, they'd met on several occasions, but the longest conversation they'd ever had was at Christy's engagement party, and that couldn't have lasted more than five minutes. Jason had been miserable in a suit and tie, and kept edging his finger along the inside of his collar as if he needed extra space to breathe properly. Actually, Jamie had spent more time that night talking to Jason than she had to Rich. Her now-husband had escorted some blonde to the elegant affair, and the woman had stayed glued to his side all evening.

A surge of irritation flashed through her. She'd never been keen on Rich's choice of women friends. She swore he could spot a bimbo a mile away.

He attracted them...Rich attracted her.

The thought raced through her mind like a Thoroughbred at top speed. Until he'd kissed her in the judge's office, Jamie had never thought of Rich in the physical, sensual way. He'd always been attractive, too handsome for his own good. But what she'd experienced earlier that afternoon had nothing to do with good looks. Instead it had a whole lot to do with sensuality.

Rich made her feel vulnerable. Exposed. Dependent. Powerless. Everything, all the emotion, all the sensations came rushing at her at once.

Afterward, he'd been so concerned. So understanding. Reassuring her fears, answering her doubts. He dried her tears with his gentleness. Turned her doubts into laughter. He'd taken the time and effort to make this day the most special of her life.

What he'd said about each of them building up the institute of marriage in their minds was true. Without realizing it, Jamie had certainly done so. She'd wanted to be married for so many years. She'd hungered for that special relationship and all that went with it, only to be left to deal with the bitter taste of one disappointment heaped on top of another.

Their dinner check arrived, and while Rich dealt with that, Jamie finished her wine. As she raised the glass to her lips, her gaze fell on the diamond on her left hand. It was a simple design, a small diamond set in the center of an antique gold rose. When Rich had first mentioned it, she hadn't felt right about wearing it, but the fit was perfect, and now that it was on her finger she was hard-pressed to remove it.

"I suppose I should drive you home."

Jamie's heart soared at the reluctance she heard in his voice. She wasn't any more eager for this day to end than he was.

"I suppose," she said with an equal lack of enthusiasm.

"You have to work tomorrow?"

Jamie nodded. "You?"

He nodded, too.

They stood, and Rich helped her put on her coat. His hands lingered on her shoulders, and he drew her back against him and breathed in deeply. "Thank you."

"For what?" Jamie wasn't sure she understood. She twisted around, and the sharp, clear restaurant sounds that surrounded them seem to fade into the distance.

"For marrying me," he whispered. "For agreeing to bear my child."

Rich bent the thick goose-down pillow in half and bunched it beneath his head. Rolling over, he glanced toward the clock radio and sighed unevenly. Nearly one. The alarm was set for five-thirty and he had yet to fall asleep.

It wasn't every day a man got married, he reminded himself. It wasn't every man who spent his wedding night alone, either.

Rich had dropped Jamie off at her condo, and although she suggested he come in for coffee, he'd refused. Hell, he didn't know why he'd turned her down. Coffee had sounded good. Damn good.

"Be honest," Rich said aloud. It wasn't the coffee that had appealed to him, it was Jamie. By the farthest stretch of the word, Jamie wasn't beautiful. But by heaven, she was appealing. It seemed impossible to him that he'd missed it all these years. Was he blind?

He'd had beautiful. Pamela was beauty-queen gorgeous—and so empty inside, so lacking in values and morals that he was left to wonder what it was about her that had attracted him in the first place. She'd appealed to his vanity, no doubt.

Rich rolled onto his back, tucked his hands beneath his head and stared up at the dark ceiling. It hadn't felt right to leave Jamie. His sense of disappointment had been keen when he'd turned around and headed for his parked car. He'd paused halfway down the stairs, resisting the urge to rush back and tell her he'd changed his mind, he'd take that coffee after all.

Instead he'd returned to an apartment that had never seemed more uninhabited and a bed that had never felt more empty.

Jamie slipped the straight skirt from her hips and clipped it to the hanger. She hung it in her closet along with the jacket and traipsed into the kitchen when the sound of the tea kettle pierced the silence.

Sitting at the table in her full-length slip, she propped her nylon-covered feet on the chair opposite her and cradled the mug of hot tea in both hands.

"I'm married," she said aloud, testing the words.

They came back empty, as empty as she felt. She hadn't wanted Rich to leave—not so soon. It was barely ten. But when she'd offered him an excuse to stay, he'd turned her down.

So this was her wedding night. In her dreams she'd built up a magical fantasy of champagne and romance. See-through nighties and wild, abandoned passion. If this were a traditional marriage, she would have all that. Instead, she'd opted for something else. Something far less.

She should be happy. Excited. In love.

She was all those things in a manner of speaking. Then why, she asked herself, did the aching loneliness weigh so heavily against her heart?

The phone on Rich's desk rang, and he automatically reached for it, not taking his eyes from the drawings he was reviewing. "Engineering."

"Hi," came the soft feminine reply.

Rich straightened. "Jamie? You're back from the doctor's already?" He checked his watch and was surprised to discover it was nearly four. He'd been involved in a project and had lost track of time.

"I just got back."

"And?" He couldn't keep the eagerness out of his voice. They'd already had one appointment to see Dr. Fullerton. Rich had gone in with Jamie for the initial visit. They had sat next to each other in Dr. Fullerton's private office and tightly held hands while the gynecologist had explained the procedure in detail.

"And," Jamie said quietly, confidently, "we're going to try for this month."

"This month," Rich repeated. "In case you didn't know this, I've always been fond of March. March is one of my most favorite months."

"Don't get too excited. It...it might not take, it doesn't generally the first try."

"April, then. April's a good month. One of my all-time favorites."

"It could easily take three or four months." Jamie laughed, the sound sweet and gentle.

"June, July and August. Who can argue with summer?" Rich found himself smiling, too. Mentally he was calculating what month the baby would be due if Jamie became pregnant in March.

"December," she said, apparently having read his silence. "How do you feel about having a December baby?"

"Jubilant. How about you?"

"It could be January or February." She sounded hesitant, as though she were afraid to put too much stock on everything coming together so smoothly for them.

"It'll happen when it happens."

"That was profound!" she said with a soft sigh. "The doctor gave me a chart. Every morning, I'm supposed to take my temperature. It will elevate slightly when I ovulate. As soon as that happens, I'm to contact his office."

"I'm going with you."

"Rich, that really isn't necessary. It's very sweet of you, but..."

"I thought you knew better than to argue with me, woman."

"I should," she said with mock exasperation. "We've been married nearly a month and I don't think I've won a single argument."

"No wonder married life agrees with me." He kept his voice low, wanting to be sure no one in the vicinity overheard him. No one other than Jason knew he'd married. "Call me in the morning," he instructed.

"Why?"

"Because, silly," he said, leaning back in his chair, "I want to keep my own chart."

The following morning, Rich was in the shower when his phone rang. He turned off the knob, grabbed a towel and raced across the bedroom.

"Hello," he greeted into the receiver.

"Ninety-eight point six."

He pulled open the drawer on his nightstand and searched blindly for a pen. Water was raining down from his hair, dripping onto the mattress. "Got it."

"I'll talk to you later."

"Great."

Wednesday morning, Rich waited in bed until he heard from her.

"Nine-eight point six." She sounded discouraged.

"Hey, nothing says it has to happen right away."

"I keep trying to visualize it."

"What is this? Think and grow pregnant?"

She laughed. "Something like that."

"Call me first thing tomorrow." He reached for his chart and made the notation.

"I will."

Thursday showed no difference, but Friday, Rich knew by the sound of her voice that something was up, and he hoped it was her temperature.

"Ninety-eight point seven . . . I think. Damn—these thermometers are difficult to read. But it's definitely higher."

Rich could envision her sitting on the edge of her bed, squinting, trying to read the infinitesimally tiny lines that marked the thermometer. He made a mental note to buy her a digital one.

"Call Dr. Fullerton."

"Rich, I'm not even sure it's elevated. It could be wishful thinking on my part."

"Call him anyway."

"If you insist."

"I do." He hung up the phone and headed toward the shower, whistling.

It wasn't until later that afternoon that the idea of taking her out to dinner came to him. Although they'd been married a month, they didn't see each other often. It had been a conscious decision on Rich's part following their wedding day. In light of what had happened when he'd kissed her, it seemed the most discerning action to take. He'd taken her to a movie the weekend following their wedding, and they'd both been ill at ease with each other. Foolish as it seemed, it was almost as if they were afraid of one another. Not once during the entire movie had they touched. Jamie didn't invite him in for coffee afterward. Even now he wasn't sure what he would have done had she offered.

They talked every day. Only last weekend he'd changed the oil in her car for her while she sewed a couple of loose buttons on his shirts for him. It was a fair exchange and afterward they'd gone out for hamburgers. Nothing fancy. The tension between them didn't seem to be as tight as when they'd attended the movie.

It was time to try again. There could well be a reason to celebrate, and a night out on the town appealed to him. Someplace special. It wasn't every day his wife's temperature was elevated by one tenth of one per cent.

Jamie was on her lunch break, and Rich didn't leave a message. He'd contact her later.

He tried again, but she was tied up with a customer. By the time he left the office, the bank was closed, so he left a message on her home answering machine.

"This is Prince Charming requesting your presence for dinner. Don't eat until you talk to me. I'm on my way home now. Call me there."

Rich fully expected a message from Jamie to be waiting for him when he arrived at his apartment. There wasn't.

He tried her again at six, six-fifteen, six-thirty and six-forty-five, leaving a message all four times.

By seven o'clock, he was concerned. A thousand possibilities crowded his mind. None of them pleasant. He paced the living room in an effort to convince himself he was overreacting, then dialed her number one last time. He listened to her recording for the sixth time, and seethed anxiously during the long piercing beep.

"Jamie, where the hell are you?" he demanded.

Chapter Six

Jamie checked her watch, keeping her wrist below the dinner table, hoping she wasn't being obvious. Eight-thirty! She'd been trapped listening to the endless details of Floyd Bacon's divorce for three solid hours.

"Don't you agree?" he asked, looking over to her.

She nodded, although she hadn't a clue what she was agreeing to. A yawn came and she attempted to swallow it, didn't succeed and tactfully pressed her fingertips to her lips. Floyd was such a nice man and she was trying hard to disguise her boredom.

"My goodness, look at the time," Floyd said.

It had all started out so innocently. Jamie had dated Floyd several years back. He was a regular customer at the bank and they'd seen each other off and on for a six-month period. Nothing serious, nothing even close to being serious. Then he'd met Carolyn and the two of them had fallen deeply in love and married. Jamie had attended their wedding. She remembered what she bought them for a wedding gift. A set of stainless-steel flatware with rosebuds emblazed on the handles, she recalled. The two had bought a house six months later. Jamie had handled the loan application for them, but when they'd moved, they'd switched their account to a branch closer to where they were living. In the past three years, Carolyn had quit work to stay home with their two young children.

"I can't tell you how sorry I am the marriage didn't work out," Jamie said, wondering what could possibly have gone wrong with two people who so obviously loved one another. Of all the couples Jamie had known over the years, she would never have suspected this would happen to Floyd and Carolyn.

"I'm sorry, too," Floyd said. His dark eyes pierced her with their sadness. He'd moved into an apartment and had stopped in at the bank to open a checking account. A new account was only an excuse, Jamie soon learned, for him to air his frustration with Carolyn, his marriage, his two preschool children and life in general.

Floyd had arrived just before closing time, lingered until he was the last customer in the bank and then suggested Jamie join him for a drink. She'd hesitated, but he'd looked so downtrodden and miserable that she'd gone against her better judgment. A drink soon turned into two and then Floyd suggested they have something to eat. At the time, it had seemed the reasonable thing to do, but that was an hour and a half earlier.

"I really should be heading home," she said, reaching for her purse. It was Friday night and the work week had seemed extra long and she was tired. Keeping track of her temperature and charting it was draining her emotional energy.

No, she decided, it was talking each morning to Rich that was responsible for that. Speaking to him first thing, discussing the intimate details of her reproductive system, hearing his enthusiasm . . . talking about their child. Nothing had prepared her for the effect all this was having. She lived day to day for those brief two-minute calls. It was almost as if he were in bed beside her . . . almost as if he were holding her in his arms. This closeness she felt toward Rich frightened her. The magnitude of what they'd done, of what they were planning, of the child they would conceive together, had brought subtle and not-so-subtle changes to their relationship.

Earlier in the day she'd hoped for and had planned to have a relaxing Friday night—to soak in a hot bubble bath and cuddle up in bed with a good book. She might have given Rich a call and invited him over for dinner. There was a new recipe she wanted to try and he seemed to enjoy her home-cooked meals. She'd only seen him twice in the past month, and it didn't seem near enough.

"I'll follow you home," Floyd said, cutting into her thoughts. He tossed some money on the table for the waitress.

It would be too late to contact Rich now. It was her turn to work Saturday morning, but she might have time to give him a call and ask him over for dinner either Saturday or Sunday. Friday nights were probably busy ones for him, it wasn't likely he'd have been home anyway.

"Jamie?"

"I'm sorry. My thoughts were a hundred miles away. There's no need for you to see me home, Floyd."

"I know, but I'd feel better if I knew you got there safely."

She nodded. Floyd really was a nice man, and she did feel terribly sorry for him. If lending a listening ear helped him, then she shouldn't complain. The time would come soon enough when she herself would need a shoulder to cry on. Once the baby was born, she'd be filing for divorce. The thought was a cheerless one.

Jamie lived less than fifteen minutes from the bank and it was on Floyd's way to his new apartment, so she didn't object strongly when he insisted upon following her.

When she pulled into her assigned parking space, he waited until she was out of her car. She waved to let him know she was safe and sound.

Floyd rolled down his car window and said, "I appreciate being able to talk to you, Jamie. You're a good friend to both Carolyn and me."

"I'm happy if I was any help."

The sadness returned to Floyd's eyes. "I really love her, you know."

Jamie nodded. She believed him. Divorce was so ugly and there was always so much pain involved. Jamie had seen more than one friend traumatized by the breakup of their marriage.

"Are you sure you really want this divorce?" she asked impulsively. Floyd looked so terribly miserable. Surely if two people deeply loved one another then they could work something out.

He shook his head. "I never did want a divorce. Carolyn's the one who... well, you know." His shoulders moved up and down with an expressive sigh.

"You're sure about that?"

Floyd hesitated. "I'm pretty sure. When I mentioned moving out, she didn't say a word to stop me. The way I figure it, if she really loved me, she would have asked me to stay."

"What if she assumed if you really loved her, you'd never want to move?"

Floyd's eyes widened as though this were a completely foreign concept. "You think that's what she might have thought?"

"I don't know, but it's worth asking, don't you think?"

"Yeah . . . I do," Floyd said, his voice revealing the first bit of enthusiasm she'd heard in him all evening. He rolled up his car window, then lowered it with a vengeance. "Jamie?"

"Yes." She was halfway toward the stairwell that led to her second-floor condominium.

"Would you mind if I used your phone? I . . . I think I'll give Carolyn a call now and see if she wants to talk. I won't stay longer than to use the phone, I promise."

"Sure." Smiling, she opened her purse and removed her key. If she'd mentioned this earlier, she might have arrived home three hours ago.

Floyd parked his car, then hurried up the stairs with her. He resembled a young boy, he was so anxious. She unlocked the door and flipped on the light switch. The minute the living room was illuminated, Floyd headed for her phone.

Jamie made herself scarce for a couple of minutes, going into her bedroom and removing her pumps. She hung up her jacket and eased the soft, smoky gray blouse from her waistband. Before leaving her bedroom, she slipped her feet into her fuzzy open-toed slippers. Then she moved into her kitchen and put the teakettle on the burner. As soon as Floyd was gone, she planned to sit back and enjoy a glass of the herb-flavored brew.

"Carolyn agrees we should talk," Floyd announced triumphantly as he replaced the telephone receiver. "She honestly sounded pleased to hear from me. Do you think she's lonely? I doubt it," he answered his own question before Jamie had the chance. "Carolyn always did have lots of friends, and she isn't one to sit home and cry in her soup, either, if you know what I mean?"

Jamie nodded. "I couldn't be more pleased for you."

"I'll be heading out then," Floyd announced triumphantly. "She's getting a sitter for the kids and she's going to meet me for a cup of coffee."

The doorbell chimed, then, in long impatient bursts. Floyd's gaze swung to Jamie. She hadn't a clue who'd be arriving this time of night.

She walked past Floyd and opened her door. No sooner had she turned the lock when Rich raced in as though he were looking to put out a fire.

"Where the hell have you been?" he demanded roughly. "I've been half out of my—" He stopped midstep and midsentence when he caught sight of Floyd. The color drained from his face, his eyes rounding with surprise, compounded by disbelief, shock and...could it be pain? Slowly he turned toward Jamie, his gaze narrowing.

"Floyd, this is Rich Manning," she said, gesturing from one to the other. "Rich, Floyd Bacon."

Floyd held out his hand, and for a moment, Jamie feared Rich wasn't going to take it. He did so reluctantly and with ill grace. "I take it Jamie didn't mention me," he said sarcastically, as though Floyd had missed the joke.

"Ah...no," Floyd said, rubbing his palms together. He eyed the front door. "Listen, I was just leaving."

"There's no need to rush," Rich said, sitting down on the sofa and crossing his long legs. He stretched his arm against the back of the cushion, giving the impression he had plenty of time to sit and chat. "I'm interested in how the two of you spent the evening." His smile lacked warmth or welcome.

"Rich," Jamie said, stepping forward. She'd never seen him like this, so sarcastic and ill-mannered.

One look from him sliced her to the quick. Rarely had she experienced a more piercing look. He looked her over, from her slippers to the blouse she'd pulled free from her waist, and his eyes narrowed, damning her.

"Jamie's an old friend," Floyd explained. "I was in the bank this afternoon and...well, you see my wife and I have separated, and Jamie—"

"So you're married, *too*."

"Too?" Frowning, Floyd looked to Jamie for an explanation.

"Yes," Rich said with a deceptively calm voice. "Jamie and I've been married...what is it now, darling, a month?"

"Rich," she warned him under her breath. He may be her legal husband, a man she'd known and respected a decade or longer, but seeing him behave like this, talk like this, he seemed like a total stranger.

"Jamie. My goodness," Floyd said, sounding thunderstruck. "You didn't say a word about having been

married. Congratulations. I wish you'd said something
earlier.''

"So do I," Rich added caustically.

Once again Floyd glanced toward the front door.
"I'd like to stay and chat, but I really need to be leaving. My wife and I are going to meet and talk . . . Jamie
was the one who suggested it. Well, actually, I came up
with the idea of calling Carolyn, but Jamie helped me
see that it was the best thing to do." He spoke rapidly,
the words coming out so fast they tumbled over one
another. "I'll be seeing you later."

Jamie held the front door open for him. "Thanks for
dinner," she said as graciously as the circumstances
would allow.

"Thanks for dinner," Rich mimicked derisively as
Floyd went out the door.

Jamie felt a storm threatening. One of anger and
frustration. The thundercloud was sitting directly behind her, and she did her level best to hold on to her in-
dignation. After taking a moment to compose herself,
she turned around. "Is something troubling you,
Rich?"

He leapt off the sofa as though he'd been sitting on a
giant spring. "Is something troubling me?" he repeated, his eyes and words frostbitten. "Just what the
hell do you think you're doing dating that joker?"

"It wasn't a date."

"I heard you thank him for dinner." He spat out the
words as though to have to say them was a detestable
task. "The least you might have done is returned my
phone calls."

"I . . . haven't checked my machine. Good grief, I
didn't arrive home until all of five minutes ago." She
hadn't had time. She did so now. Moving across the

room, she pressed down the switch. A list of six messages, all from Rich, played back, each sounding progressively less patient and increasingly anxious. The last one had been to demand to know "where the hell" she was.

"When I couldn't stand waiting for the phone to ring, I drove over here to wait for you. Low and behold, your car was in your space and you were here...with Floyd."

"I can understand your concern," Jamie said calmly, willing to grant him that much.

"You're my wife, dammit. How am I supposed to feel when you turn up missing?" He forcefully raked his fingers through his hair and stalked to the far side of the room.

Standing next to her answering machine, her back stiff, Jamie drew in a soothing breath, determined this wouldn't evolve into a full-fledged argument. "I was never missing. I'm sorry I worried you, Rich, but you're overreacting, and frankly, it's beginning to annoy me."

"Annoy *you?* I've been pacing the floor for the past three hours...."

"I would have phoned."

"You brought a man home with you!" He made it sound as though that were grounds for divorce.

"Floyd is an old friend."

The teakettle whistled, the sound splitting the silence like an ax hacking through the center of a dry log. Jamie hurried into the kitchen and removed it from the stove. The boiling water bubbled from the spout, nearly scalding her. Rich followed behind her.

"Apparently you don't have a problem letting *old friends* take you out to dinner," he accused her, his words inflamed with impatience.

Jamie gritted her teeth, biting back an angry retort. "He needed a sounding board, someone who would listen to his problems. You're making it sound as though I did something underhanded. I was just being a friend."

"You're a married woman," Rich bellowed. He slammed his hand against the counter. "*My* wife. How do you think it makes me feel, knowing you chose to go out to dinner with another man instead of your own husband?"

"I didn't choose Floyd over you. Good heavens, how was I supposed to know you wanted to take me to dinner? I'm not a mind reader."

"If you'd come home after work the way you're supposed to, you would have heard the first of my six messages."

"That's ridiculous. I can't run my life according to your whims." She was doing an admirable job of keeping her temper intact, but she didn't know how much longer her precarious hold would last.

"I thought you were different." A spark of pain flashed in his eyes.

"What do you mean by that?"

"I would have trusted you with my life, but you're like every other woman I've ever known. The minute my back is turned, you think nothing of seeing someone else."

The emptiness in his voice cut at Jamie's tender heart. "That's so unfair."

"We're legally married, and even that didn't make a difference." His voice sounded like thunder echoing through her kitchen, slapping sound against the walls. His eyes, once so blue and beautiful, pierced her with accusations.

"This isn't a real marriage and you know it," she argued heatedly. Her voice was shaking with the effort to keep from shouting. "You were the one who insisted on the ceremony, but it was for convenience's sake."

"We're married!"

"Maybe so, but that doesn't give you the right to storm into my home and insult my guests."

"I'll do as I damn well please. You have no right bringing a man home with you."

"That's ridiculous." Jamie couldn't believe they were having this conversation. It was ludicrous. "The marriage is in name only for... for obvious reasons."

"We said our vows."

"Don't remind me." The promises they'd made to one another continued to haunt her.

"Clearly someone has to."

"Oh-h-h." Jamie seethed. Tightening her fists at her side, she exhaled sharply and resisted the urge to open and close her cupboard doors to vent her frustration.

"Temper, temper."

"I think you'd better leave before we say something we'll regret." Her instincts had told her that getting married wouldn't work, and she'd refused to listen to them. Now she was suffering the consequences.

"Not on your life."

"This is my home," Jamie cried, quickly losing her grip on her rage. She'd never known Rich could be so unreasonable, so rude, so... impossible.

"You're just like every other woman I've ever known," Rich repeated in unflattering tones.

"And you're just like every other man, so wrapped up in your ego that it'd take a two-by-four across the side of your head before you could see what's right in front of your nose."

"It wasn't me who went out behind your back," he shouted. He leaned against the kitchen counter and crossed his arms as though to suggest that a bulldozer would have trouble budging him.

"Why do you care if I had dinner with a dozen men?" she demanded. "It never bothered you before!"

"We weren't married before."

"I'm not your possession," she challenged. "You have no right, husband or not, telling me who I can and cannot see."

"The hell I don't."

Jamie squeezed her eyes closed in abject frustration. "I knew this wasn't going to work...I told you it wouldn't, but would you listen? Oh, no, you knew so much better."

"I still do."

Jamie couldn't help it, she stamped her foot. She hadn't done anything so childish since junior high. The man was driving her insane.

"Look at us," she cried, her voice shaking with anger and regret. "I'm...I'm not pregnant yet and already we're fighting. We're going to ruin everything fighting over something that's...stupid."

"It isn't stupid to me."

"Floyd is just a friend. For heaven's sake, he's married."

"So are you."

"Why are you doing this?" she cried.

"All I'm asking is that you keep your side of the bargain and I'll keep mine. That shouldn't be so difficult."

"Oh, right," she said, walking around the table and bracing her hands against the back of a chair. "There's a whole lot more involved in this arrangement than I ever knew about or agreed to and—"

"Like what?"

"Like . . . your caveman attitude toward me."

"Caveman? Because I don't want my wife dating another man—another *married* man?" He glared across the room at her. "Forgive me if I'm wrong, but I seem to remember there being a phrase or two in the wedding vows that state—"

"Don't you dare." Jamie pointed her index finger at his chest as though she was aiming a derringer and one false move would cost him his life. "Don't you dare," she repeated. "I never wanted to go through with the wedding ceremony and you knew it. Using it against me now is the height of unfairness."

"We're married, Jamie, whether you like it or not."

"I don't like it. . . . I hate it. I hate everything about it—it's the biggest mistake of my life." Unable to bear arguing any longer, she whirled around and covered her face with her hands. If there were any decency left in him, Rich Manning would leave her in peace.

Static electricity filled the kitchen, crackling, arcing from one end of the room to the other. The silence was deafening. More deafening than any explosion.

Jamie's nerves were raw, the hair at her nape bristled as she heard Rich move. The sound of his footsteps told her he was coming toward her. The clipped pace of his steps did nothing to reassure her.

"Did he kiss you?"

"No!" she shouted, furious he would ask such an outrageous question.

"Good, because I'm going to." His hands moved over her shoulders, cupping them.

At his words, her nipples tightened and the blood rushed into her face. "No," she made one weak protest, but she didn't know who she was speaking to, Rich or herself. He'd kissed her once, the day of their wedding, and it had haunted her every moment since. She couldn't allow him to destroy her equilibrium again, destroy her peace of mind.

Although she resisted, Rich twisted her around. Jamie's face was on fire... her body was on fire, and he'd barely touched her. She struggled, jerking her shoulders back and forth, but her effort was futile.

Rich grabbed hold of her chin, his fingers imprisoning her, yet his touch was oddly gentle. Without a word more, he bent down and smothered her mouth with his own. Jamie knew she shouldn't allow him to do this. Not in the heat of anger. Not when they were fighting. Not when his kiss would only create a need for more.

He tasted so damn good, so damn wonderful. It wasn't fair. Nothing about this arrangement seemed to be.

He moved his mouth over hers, shaping her lips with his own, grinding them back and forth until she weakened and moaned in protest. It seemed to be what he was waiting for. The instant her lips parted, his tongue swept inside like a mighty conqueror marching through the gates of Rome.

Shock waves vibrated through her at the small, ruthless movement of his tongue. Jamie could feel herself melting against him. She was incredibly hot, incredibly needy. The need continued to build within her, licking at her senses, growing hotter and stronger and more fierce with every foray of his tongue.

Not satisfied with her lips alone, he kissed her eyes and her throat, until Jamie felt as if she were about to ignite from spontaneous combustion.

A frightening excitement exploded inside her, going beyond mere pleasure and quickly advancing to a demand so hungry, so strong that there would be no turning back for either of them.

"Rich...no," she protested, bracing her hands against his chest, wanting to use that as leverage to break away. He was too angry with her, too frustrated to fully realize what he was doing.

"Yes," he countered with a groan. His arms encircled her waist, and he effortlessly lifted her from the floor, adjusting her hips flush against his own so she was graphically aware of what she was doing to him. Of how great his own need for her was.

In her heart, Jamie recognized no good would come of this, but it felt too damn wonderful to stop now. She looped her arms around his neck, slanted her head and kissed him back, giving him her tongue. She felt famished beyond reason, impoverished and wanton.

A low, rough sound rumbled from deep within his throat.

"Rich...please, oh, please, we've got to stop." Her heart was reeling with excitement like a plate spinning at the end of a long thin stick.

"Not yet." He pressed his lips to her neck, running the tip of his tongue across the smooth, silky skin of her throat and up the underside of her jaw. Jamie eased back her head to grant him fuller access. A ribbon of warm pleasure braided its way down her spine.

She buried her fingers in his hair and sighed, feeling both breathless and hot. So breathless she could barely catch her wind. So very hot. Hotter than she could ever remember being.

He lifted her higher, edging her buttocks onto the top of the kitchen counter. His hands worked the buttons of her blouse, effortlessly peeling it from her shoulders. Her bra clasped in the back, and he made a rough, growllike sound as he reached for and found the hook.

Jamie knew she should protest, put an end to this madness before it consumed them both, but she longed to bare her breasts to him. For years he'd teased her, and all along he had no idea. None. Her breasts were full. Ripe and lush.

Most important, they were his.

Deftly he unfastened the hook and drew the tiny slip of lace down her arms. He paused when the journey was half made. Jamie gloried in the way his eyes rounded with surprise and wonder. Slowly he lifted his gaze to hers as though he wasn't sure she was real.

His lips, warm and moist, slid across the heaviness of one breast, then fastened on the beaded nipple. Jamie moaned and closed her eyes. The pleasure was so intense that it bordered on pain. The tension slowly coiled within her until it was so hot she feared she'd soon burn out of control.

"Jamie." Her name was a groan coming from his lips. His hands bunched her breasts together, and he buried his face in their fullness.

"I know." He didn't need to speak for her to know what he was saying. They'd gone as far as they dare without making love, without her leading him into her bed and surrendering everything to the magic of his touch.

Mindlessly, she arched her back.

He moaned once more between clenched teeth. "I want you."

She wanted him, too, but it would only lead to more problems and they were already dealing with more than they could handle. Making love would destroy them. They'd both agreed to as much before the wedding.

He dropped his hands to her thighs, edging up the material of her skirt one tantalizing inch at a time. "Tell me what you want," he demanded, slipping his hands over her nylon-covered thighs, stroking them while he spread a layer of delicate, moist kisses across her neck.

"I . . . don't know."

"Funny, I do," he countered with a lazy, sexy laugh. "You want me."

Jamie couldn't deny it. She could barely speak as a powerful coil of need tightened within her.

"Deny it." The tip of his tongue moistened a trail across the underside of her jaw.

"I can't."

"Me, either." He scooted her from the counter, shifting her weight until she was completely in his arms. He carried her as if she weighed nothing at all and headed out of the kitchen. He paused to turn off the light.

"Rich." She had to say something before it was too late. "We'll regret this in the morning." Even as she spoke, she wound her arms around his neck.

"Maybe." He didn't bother to deny it, but it didn't stop him, either.

Her bedroom was dark. Moonlight splashed across the top of her bed, and Rich slowly lowered her onto the mattress.

There was no turning back now.

Chapter Seven

Jamie's eyes were wild as she stared up at him. Rich was aware of every breath she drew. The sweet rise and fall of her chest enthralled him, as did her pulse. It throbbed madly at the base of her throat. He stepped away from her and tugged the sweater over his head, bunched it in his hand and tossed it aside. His pants were next, then his briefs, until he stood before her. He could sense and could feel the tension pulsating through her, but she did nothing to stop him.

He placed his hands on her waist and with her help stripped what remained of her clothes, treating them as carelessly as his own. He was so damn eager for her, he was shaking. Maybe she was right and they'd regret this in the morning, but he'd deal with his feelings then. For now he was going to immerse himself in the pleasure they both craved so desperately.

Rich eased onto the mattress beside her. Jamie was on her side and he positioned himself so he was facing her. She slid her flattened hands up his chest, her touch light, tentative, as though she were afraid.

Rich's heart was pounding, a giant piston inside his chest, the sound of it so strong it echoed like thunder in his ear. He had to taste her again, had to experience once again the addictive sweetness of her kiss. With limitless patience, he eased her mouth to his.

The kiss was slow and deep and thorough. Hot excitement churned through him until he thought he would explode with it. Breaking off the kiss, he lifted his face away from her and drew in a deep, sharp breath.

"You taste good."

"You do, too," she whispered. Her fingers were in his hair, urging his mouth back to her own. Their tongues met, darting around each other, exploring, tasting, sparring. Suddenly the kiss was neither slow nor patient, but urgent and demanding, so demanding he was frightening himself with the fiery need he felt for her.

"It's not supposed to be this good," she whimpered.

"Yes, it is." He rolled her onto her back and positioned himself between her legs. "It's going to get even better."

Rich knew he'd find it impossible to wait a minute longer. His entire body was throbbing. Jamie bent her knees and arched her back to him, her thighs nestling his hips. Their eyes met and held in the golden glow of the moonlight. Slowly, frightened by the strength of desire that surged through him, Rich guided himself into position and began to enter her.

She was hot and moist and incredibly tight. By the time he had buried himself to the hilt inside her, he was panting at the intensity of pleasure.

He loved her and he needed her. All these years he'd been so blind to what was right in front of him. What Jamie said about hitting him over the head with a two-by-four had been right, only he'd been deaf to her words. He'd been nearly insane with worry when he hadn't been able to reach her. When he'd found her with Floyd, he'd behaved like a jealous idiot. Rich had never been more jealous in his life. He'd wanted to tear the other man limb from limb.

"Ohhh, Rich," Jamie moaned.

"I'm hurting you."

"No... no. It's just so good."

He began to move, slowly at first, gaining rhythm, controlling his thrusts, determined to prolong the pleasure, feed his growing need and desire for her. Jamie met each lunge, arching her body upward, lifting her hips, welcoming him, taking him in even deeper. They strained together, muscles trembling, their breathing harsh and rapid, in perfect unison.

As he buried himself inside her, the hair on his chest brushed against her breasts, her hardened nipples searing him. When he could bear the teasing no longer, he paused and lowered his mouth to her breast, the need to taste her too urgent to ignore. He moistened both nipples, wetting them with his tongue, sucking at them gently until she moaned softly and buckled beneath him.

"Rich..." Her long nails dug into his flexing muscles.

Rich responded by gripping hold of her hips and lifting her, fitting himself most solidly inside her, rocking with her in a cadence, a meter that left him writhing on the verge of the most profound pleasure he'd ever experienced.

"Jamie..." The hottest fever imaginable claimed him.

"Yes...oh, Rich, yes," she sobbed as she thrashed wildly beneath him.

His climax came, drowning him in a pleasure so keen it went beyond description. A pleasure so acute he might have died in that second and suffered no regrets.

They were silent afterward, their breathing labored and hard, their chests heaving against one another. Rich wished Jamie would say something, anything. She didn't, and slowly reality returned, unexplainably linked with the wonder and the glory of what they'd shared.

Rich kissed her softly, gently, with none of the urgency he'd felt earlier. He slid his fingers into the silky length of her hair and sighed with satisfaction. He kissed her again, reveling in the warm, sweet taste of her. He longed for her to ease his mind, tell him she experienced no remorse over their lovemaking. He'd been so angry, and one thing had led to another, and before he could stop it from happening they were making love. She'd warned him, claimed they'd be left to deal with regrets, but he felt none. Only a powerful sense of honesty.

Rich realized his weight was too much for her, but when he went to move, she resisted, tightening her hold on him, hooking her ankles over his.

"Don't leave me."

"No." He had no intention of doing so. "I'm too heavy for you."

"Stay with me like this. Please." She stroked his back, her touch light, gentle.

He would stay because she asked, but only for a little while before he fell asleep and smothered her with his weight. It felt wonderful to remain inside her, to soak in her softness, drink in the sweet contentment.

The moonlight softly illuminated her face. He noticed her eyes were languorous, her face flushed pink with pleasure. Her lips were turned up slightly in a secret, womanly smile of serenity. Just watching her, loving her, did funny things to Rich's heart. The love he felt for her burned within his chest, literally burned with the depth of emotion he felt.

Her skin felt like silk beneath his hands as he brushed his fingertips down the side of her face. She sighed, and her breath caught in her throat.

Rarely had Rich experienced such contentment. The magnitude of it left him feeling weak and humble. Jamie's womanly body, so soft, silky and moist, sheathed him. The unique scent she wore wafted its way around his heart and mind. Tucking his arms securely around her waist, he rolled onto his back, taking her with him. She made a small sound of surprise, then smiled peacefully, nestled her head upon his broad chest and closed her eyes. Within minutes, she was sound asleep.

Slumber didn't claim him as quickly. He remained in awe of the wealth of emotion that crowded his heart. For years he'd been blind, deaf and dumb when it came to his feelings for Jamie. Others saw it. James had recognized the love Rich felt for her and said as much. Rich had been quick to laugh and deny what was obvious to everyone but himself.

It had taken a heated argument to push him over the edge, push them both past the point of no return. If he had any regrets, it was that this discovery had come on the heels of a heated exchange.

Closing his eyes, he sighed and ran his hand down the nest of curls crowning Jamie's head. She slept, utterly content, and his heart swelled with a love so strong it was all he could do not to wake her and tell her everything he was feeling. He wanted to, but it would be selfish to take advantage of her fatigue. He kissed her temple, and closed his eyes, content to keep his wife securely wrapped in his arms.

Sometime toward dawn, Rich woke. Jamie was sleeping on her side and he was cuddling her, their bodies intimately pressing against one another. A smile worked at his heart. They were like an old married couple, completely comfortable with one another, as though they'd been sleeping together for years on end.

This was exactly what Rich intended, to continue sleeping with Jamie night after night for the remainder of their lives. They were an old married couple. Well, not old, but they'd grow that way, gracefully, together. God willing, they'd raise several children, who'd be secure in the love their parents shared.

Rich stirred once more a little after six. Yawning, he stretched his arms high above his head. He'd been working a lot of extra hours on a military contract Boeing had with the government.

He slipped out of bed and gazed down on Jamie. His heart swelled with love, and he leaned over, gently kissed her forehead and headed for the shower, whistling a cheerful tune.

In a joyous mood, Rich sang at the top of his lungs. He half expected Jamie to be awake once he returned but was disappointed to discover she remained asleep. He dressed and headed out the door. He would phone her later, once he got the chance. He had a tendency to get busy and forget about the time, but he'd make the effort not to let that happen. They had to talk.

Jamie woke at eight. Although she was sleeping on her side, facing the wall, she sensed almost immediately that Rich had gone.

He'd abandoned her without a word. Left her to deal with the emptiness of the morning. Alone.

Squeezing her eyes closed, she bit into her lower lip. The feeling of betrayal, of total isolation she experienced was matchless to nothing she'd ever experienced.

Their argument played back in her mind, over and over in slow motion. Every ugly word they'd said to each other, the accusations, the hurt, echoed within her mind as if they'd been shouted against a canyon wall, taunting her again and again.

His reaction from the night before made perfect sense in the bright light of morning. It must have been more than his pride could take to find her with Floyd. Something inside Rich had cracked and given way.

Her evening with Floyd, no matter how innocent, must have been a slap in Rich's face. He'd reacted in anger and pain, not because he was jealous, or because he cared. The reason for his outburst was directly related to his strong male ego. What had started out as an argument had eventually progressed to a physical reaction.

Rich had kissed her. First in anger. Then in need. A need fed by his frustration and annoyance. He hadn't been jealous. Not really.

The image of her husband, standing in her kitchen, was unforgettable. He'd been furious with her. Although her back had been turned away from him at the time, she knew she'd outraged him when she told him their marriage had been the biggest mistake of her life.

A terrible tension had followed, so impenetrable that Jamie doubted she could have said or done anything to have relieved it. Sitting up in bed, Jamie pushed the hair away from her face.

Rich hadn't kissed her for any of the right reasons. He'd done it because he hadn't believed her. He assumed Floyd had kissed her, and his pride couldn't bear to have another woman cheat on him. Cheat, even if it was only in his imagination.

All the years of their friendship, Jamie had distinguished Rich from the other men she'd known. That had been the first of several mistakes. Rich was exactly like the others, competitive and territorial.

A few weeks earlier he'd attempted to set her up with his engineering friend, Bill whatever-his-name-was. Now Rich couldn't tolerate her speaking to another man, even someone as blameless as Floyd Bacon. Good grief, Floyd was a married man. Did Rich honestly think she'd stoop to that level? Apparently he did, which didn't speak well of his opinion of her.

She'd never seen Rich more unreasonable. He'd refused to listen to her explanation, had been rude and arrogant to the extreme. And for what reason? None! At least none that she could understand.

What he'd said about them being married was true enough, on paper. But their relationship wasn't any different now than it had been before the ceremony.

Only it was. Everything she'd feared was coming to pass.

They'd been married a month, and look what had happened. It wouldn't be nearly as tragic if Rich hadn't left her to face the morning alone. The questions tormented her, clipping away at her pride and self-confidence.

If only he'd said something afterward.

If only she'd said something.

It had all been so beautiful. The wonder of their lovemaking had captured her heart, her soul.

Jamie had longed to tell him everything she was feeling, but she'd been afraid. Afraid he hadn't experienced the same wonder. Afraid he'd be embarrassed. Afraid he was suffering with regrets. She couldn't have beared knowing that, not when everything had been so perfect for her.

Evidently he'd had second thoughts, otherwise he wouldn't have abandoned her, slipping away like a thief in the night.

Leaving her to face the morning alone.

Reluctantly, her heart heavy, Jamie climbed out of bed and into the shower. The pulsating spray beat against her skin like dull needles. The need to release her anguish in the form of tears left her throat aching and raw, but she refused to cry. She didn't have the time. It was her turn to work the Saturday morning shift at the bank. She was already behind schedule.

With a towel wrapped around her middle, she traipsed back into her bedroom, and hesitated. She covered her cheeks with her hands, mortified to discover her carelessly discarded clothes tossed from one end of the room to the other. The memory of how eager they'd been for each other added a hundredfold to her humiliation.

Jamie dressed quickly, then hung her clothes from the night before in the farthest reaches of her closet and hurried out the door, not bothering with more than a cup of instant coffee.

* * *

Rich tried phoning Jamie at a quarter to ten. Surely she'd be up and about by then. The phone rang three times. Before the answering machine could connect, he hung up. He'd sung his song to that recorder of hers more than he cared to remember. He would try again later, he promised himself.

It was noon before he had a chance to get away a second time. When she didn't answer, he become irritated and set the receiver down harder than he intended.

"Problems?" Bill Hastings asked, walking into Rich's office.

"Not really." He did his best to appear relaxed.

"Don't try to kid me," Bill said, sitting on the corner of Rich's desk, his left foot dangling. "I know the look when I see it, I've worn it often enough myself. You've got women problems."

It wouldn't do any good to deny it, so he said nothing.

"Pamela again?"

"Not this time."

Bill's eyebrows shot upward. "Someone else? You've been lying low lately. I didn't know you were seeing anyone else."

"I'm not exactly." It was a half truth, which also made it a half lie. He wasn't seeing anyone. He was a married man, only Bill didn't know that and Rich wasn't in any mood to announce the news now. Not when he didn't know what the hell was going on between him and Jamie.

Everything had been good for them. Every time he thought about their lovemaking, his head spun and he felt tender and warm inside. It wasn't a sensation he was comfortable with, nor was it something he'd experienced in other relationships.

He'd thought, at least he'd hoped Jamie had shared in the magic they'd created, but apparently that wasn't the case. It astonished him that he could have misread her so completely.

At two, Rich decided to try reaching Jamie one last time. He might be reading a whole lot more into her not answering the phone than she intended. She might not be there to answer it. From his own experience, he knew Saturdays were often busy with errands.

He'd phone again and if there wasn't any answer, then the hell with it. A man had his pride.

He'd wait until she called him.

The phone was ringing when Jamie, struggling with a bag of groceries, tried to remove the key from her purse and unlatch her front door. Once the lock was free, she threw open the door and raced across the room, praying with everything in her that it was Rich.

"Hello," she cried breathlessly after making a death leap for the phone. Whoever it was had apparently just disconnected the line and a buzz droned in her ear.

She knew without question that the caller hadn't been Rich. He'd left six or more messages on her answering machine the night before. He wouldn't be shy about leaving another.

On the off chance he had, she pressed the button to her machine and listened impatiently while it played back all the ones she had yet to erase.

Nothing new from Rich. Nothing.

The emptiness around her seemed to swell, expanding to suffocating proportions. Her heart felt like a lead weight inside her chest as she walked across her living room and closed the front door. The bag of groceries had been tossed on the sofa as she'd dashed for the phone. The apples had tumbled from the bag, spilling onto the cushions along with a box of cold cereal and a bottle of imported wine.

Like a romantic fool, she'd gone out and purchased an expensive bottle of wine. Her morning had been hectic—Saturdays at the bank generally were. But no matter how many customers she had served, or how many loan applications she had reviewed, Jamie hadn't been able to stop thinking about Rich.

He wasn't like other men she'd known. She'd loved him far too long to condemn him on such flimsy evidence. There were any number of logical reasons he might have had to leave. She was a sound sleeper, and for all she knew he could have tried to wake her. By the time she left the bank at a little after one, Jamie was convinced she'd hear from Rich. Confident enough for her to rush out and buy a bottle of wine and a small sirloin tip roast just so she could invite him over to dinner—so they could talk.

There was so much they needed to say.

Rich stared at the phone accusingly, willing it to ring. He'd arrived home late Saturday afternoon. He was in such a rush to listen to the messages on his answering machine that he didn't stop to check his mail. He bounded up the stairs to his apartment, taking two and three steps at a time, convinced there'd be some word from Jamie waiting for him.

The blinking red light on his answering machine had eased the tension between his shoulder blades. Rich had felt almost cocky with relief. Until he played the message, that is, and discovered it was Jason who had phoned. Jason and not Jamie. His brother, not his wife.

So this was what it meant to be married, to wear his heart on his sleeve and mope around like a besotted fool. So this was what it felt like to truly love another. To constantly wage war against frustration, to walk one day into the next battling disappointment. To care so damn much that his whole life hinged on a single phone call.

Rich was through waiting. He'd already ruined one night pacing the floors like a madman yearning to hear from Jamie. He'd be damned before he'd do it again anytime soon.

Furthermore, he mused darkly, he was through allowing a woman to rule his heart and his head. Apparently he hadn't learned his lesson.

Pamela had stuck a ring through his nose and strung him along for weeks. He'd played the clown for one woman and he wasn't eager to do so again. Not even for Jamie.

If she was foolish enough to throw away the best thing that had ever happened to the two of them, then so be it. The choice rested entirely with her and he wasn't going to say a word to persuade her one way or another. Not a single word.

Clearly she felt none of the beauty of their night together. None of the wonder and the magic. It stung his pride that he could have misread her so completely.

Rather than dwell on his marriage, Rich reached for the phone and punched out his older brother's number with a vengeance. Jason answered on the second ring, and the two made plans for the evening. Nothing fancy. Paul, their eldest brother, had invited them over for a round-robin of pinochle. Cards sounded a hell of a lot more inviting than sitting home all night waiting for a silent phone to ring.

Call him. Jamie had never spent a more restless Saturday afternoon and evening in her life. Pride, she soon discovered, made for mighty poor company.

For all she knew, he could be just as eagerly waiting for her to contact him. But that made no sense to her, especially since he'd been the one to slip away in the early morning hours. Even so, she was willing to give him the benefit of the doubt. More than willing. Eagerly willing.

Although her stomach was in knots, she'd gone about cooking an elaborate dinner, just in case Rich did phone. The roast and small red potatoes made a perfect excuse to invite him over. Now the meal sat on top of her stove untouched. Unappreciated. Forsaken. Just as she was.

When she could bear the silence no longer, Jamie reached for the phone. Her hand was trembling and she paused to clear her throat twice while she was dialing. She forced herself to smile, determined to sound as chipper as a robin in springtime when Rich answered the phone.

Only he didn't.

After four long rings, his machine came on.

Jamie was so stunned, she listened for a couple of seconds, then with a heart-aching reluctance, disconnected the telephone line. For several moments, her hand remained on the receiver as the futility and the discouragement overwhelmed her.

It was silly of her. Asinine. Naive. But it had never occurred to her, not once, that Rich wouldn't be home.

Apparently he'd gone out for the evening. No doubt he was having fun, laughing it up with his friends, enjoying himself while she sat home and twiddled her thumbs.

There were places for her to go, people to see, fun to be had by her, as well. She contacted three friends and suggested a movie. It was a sad testimony to her life that the most exciting form of entertainment she could think to suggest was a movie.

All three of her friends already had plans for the evening, which was just as well since Jamie wasn't all that keen to go out anyway. It was the kind of night when she was destined to sit and watch reruns on television with a box of crackers in her lap and a six-pack of diet soda to keep her company.

Rich had a great time Saturday night. They'd played cards well into the early hours of the morning and thoroughly enjoyed themselves. For a while Rich had completely forgotten Jamie. There'd been whole stretches of time he didn't think of her once. Five- and ten-minute blocks of time.

Things would have gone well if it hadn't been for Jason. Damn but his brother enjoyed walking close to the edge.

"So how's the marriage of *in*convenience working out?" he'd asked on the drive home. He made it sound like one big joke, but Rich wasn't in a laughing mood.

Rather than go into any of the sorry details of his marriage, Rich gave an unintelligible reply.

"What's that?" Jason pressed.

"I didn't say anything."

"I know."

"Just drop it, Jason." Rich was serious and he made sure his brother knew it. He didn't want to discuss his relationship with Jamie. Not then, and perhaps not for a good long while. What she'd said the night before about their marriage being the worst mistake of her life was beginning to have a ring of truth to it.

"So," Jason added after a few minutes, "marriage isn't exactly a bed of roses the way you'd hoped."

"I never claimed it would be."

"Is she pregnant yet?"

"Pregnant?" Jason repeated the word as though he'd never heard it before. "Pregnant," he said again, his voice dropping several decibels. Vividly he recalled their conversation Friday morning and how excited he'd been when he learned her temperature had been slightly elevated. They'd spoken every morning several days running, discussing a pregnancy. It was the reason they were married! Only, they'd planned to conceive the child in nontraditional methods. . . .

Twenty-four hours following his conversation with his brother, Rich's mind continued to mull over the prospect of Jamie and the possibility of a pregnancy.

Rich hadn't heard from Jamie all day Sunday, either. He'd decided he probably wouldn't. Damn but that woman was stubborn. Fine, he'd wait her out. If she didn't contact him, then it was her loss.

He changed his mind Monday afternoon. It was either contact her or resign from his engineering job. He'd made one mistake after another all day. Every time the phone rang, it was as though an electrical shock went through him. He nearly leaped off his chair. Although he strove to sound cool and collected, he couldn't keep his heart from speeding like a race-car engine.

* * *

It was apparent he would have to be the one to call her. Rich felt as though he'd been blackmailed, which did little to improve his mood. After mulling over his options, he stood and closed the door to his office.

He walked all the way around his desk twice before he realized what he was doing. Then, as though he feared someone would guess his unrest, he scooted out his chair and sat back down.

The receptionist for the bank answered almost immediately.

"Is Jamie...Warren available?" he asked gruffly. He stopped himself just in time. He'd nearly requested to speak to Jamie Manning. Not once had he linked his name with hers, although they were married. Now it seemed unnatural to call her by her maiden name.

"I'll ring her desk," the woman said, cutting him off. The phone pealed three times, frustrating Rich even more. Did the woman have built-in sonar so she'd know when it was him calling?

"This is Jamie Warren's desk. How may I help you?"

"Ah..." Rich had expected Jamie would answer. "Is Jamie available?"

"No, I'm sorry, she's home sick today. May I be of service?"

"Ah..." Jamie was home sick? She'd seemed in perfect enough health Friday night. Perhaps she was seriously ill. Too ill to contact him.

"Sir? May I help you?"

"No...no, thanks, I'll phone back later."

But first he was going to find out exactly what was wrong with Jamie.

Get 4 Books FREE

SEE BACK OF CARD FOR DETAILS

Chapter Eight

Jamie felt utterly wretched. Not only had she spent the most miserable weekend of her life, but late Sunday afternoon she'd come down with a ferocious case of the flu.

Monday morning there'd been no help for it and she'd phoned in sick. For most of the day she'd stayed in bed curled up in a fetal position, trying to convince herself it was a twenty-four-hour virus and that she'd be fine by Tuesday morning.

Her head throbbed, her muscles ached and she was certain she was running a high fever. If she wasn't so sick, she'd get out of bed and take her temperature. The only times she'd risked leaving the comfort of her warm cocoon had been to take an express trip to her bathroom.

The phone rang at her bedside and she blindly reached for it, nearly toppling a glass of liquid flu medication leftover from the night before.

"Hello." No doubt it was some salesman looking to sell her a cemetery plot. The timing couldn't be more perfect.

"Jamie?"

"Rich?" Naturally he'd phone her now, when her defenses were down and she was too weak to react. She'd waited three tortuous days to hear from him. Nightmare days.

Now that he had called, Jamie experienced zero emotion. Certainly not relief. Nor anger, although she'd spent the better part of Sunday furious with him, and so hurt it was all she could do not to immerse herself in pity.

"I phoned the bank and they told me you were home ill," he explained, as though he needed a reason to contact her.

"I've got the flu."

A slight hesitation followed. "You're sure? Have you been to the doctor?"

"I'm too sick for that." She found his concern laughable. He'd walked out on her. Ignored her. Hurt her. And now he was upset because she hadn't seen a doctor over a twenty-four-hour bug.

Once again Rich hesitated. "I think you should make an appointment with Dr. Fullerton."

"Dr. Fullerton?" she echoed. Rich made no sense whatsoever. "Why in heaven's name would I see a gynecologist?"

"Because what you have might not be the flu," he returned, his low words sounding as though they were issued from between clenched teeth.

Maybe she was being obtuse, but she just didn't follow his line of thought. "Trust me, it's the flu. I've got all the symptoms."

"Did it dawn on you that it might be something else?" His voice rose with impatience.

"No. Should it?"

"Dammit, yes!"

It hit Jamie then with the force of a lightening bolt. She had been dull-witted, but not intentionally. Rich thought she might be pregnant! If it wasn't so ludicrous she'd cry. He actually sounded worried.

"It's too soon to tell," she said in her most formal-sounding voice, as if she were relaying the bank's decision regarding a loan application. "But it's unlikely."

"Your temperature was elevated, remember?"

"Not that much. Don't worry, you're safe."

The rough sound of his angry sigh vibrated over the telephone wire. Either he was greatly exasperated or furious—Jamie couldn't tell which.

When would she learn? Time after time she'd foolishly handed her heart to a man, and the outcome was always the same. Within a few months she limped away licking her wounds. There were some women who were meant to find love, but apparently she wasn't one of them. Some women were destined to live forty or fifty years of contented marital bliss. Her marriage would be lucky to last two months.

"Do you need anything?" Rich asked.

"No." She made her reply as clipped as she could. If he really cared, he wouldn't have left her Saturday to face the morning alone. "I'm perfectly fine."

"Then why weren't you at work?"

"Because I've got the flu," she argued, hating the way they each took pains to guard their fragile egos.

"You aren't *perfectly fine* then, are you?"

How like a man to argue the point. "Other than the flu, I'm feeling absolutely wonderful." She tried to make it sound as though she'd be out stacking logs if it weren't for this pesky virus. There certainly wasn't anything in her life that was causing her any concern, other than an almost-husband who took delight in walking all over her heart.

"We need to talk," Rich suggested after an awkward moment. The silence was strained between them— as strained as their marriage.

Jamie couldn't agree more. "I...think that might be a good idea."

"When?"

"Ah..." Jamie wasn't sure. Not anytime soon with the pitiful way she was feeling. If she looked even close to as dreadful as she felt, Rich would personally cart her into Dr. Fullerton's office.

"Wednesday night?" Rich suggested, sounding impatient, as though she were purposely putting him off.

"Wednesday...sure." By then she should be well on the road to recovery.

"The Cookie Jar?"

The restaurant was one they'd frequented while in high school. A little hole-in-the-wall place with a polished linoleum floor and an old-time jute box in the corner. Jamie hadn't thought about the soda shop in years. "I didn't know they were still in business."

"I was driving down Forty-third recently and saw it was there. It brought back a lot of old memories. If you'd rather meet somewhere else..."

"No, The Cookie Jar sounds like it might be fun. I'll meet you there at...how does seven sound?"

"Fine. At seven. I'll buy you a chocolate sundae."

Despite everything she'd been through the last three days—the anxiety, the disappointment, and the pain—Jamie found herself smiling. A few words from Rich wiped it all away. "I'll let you."

He chuckled. "Somehow I knew you would."

A couple of moments later, Jamie replaced the telephone receiver and nestled back on the thick goosedown pillows. She'd been chilled earlier and had piled every blanket in the house on top of her. She was feeling much better now though. Good enough to climb out of bed and make herself something to eat.

Wednesday, Rich arrived at The Cookie Jar an hour early. He slipped into the red booth with tattered vinyl upholstery and reached for the menu, which was tucked between the napkin holder and the sugar container. The plastic-coated menu offered four or five varieties of hamburgers, in addition to sandwiches and a wide range of ice-cream desserts. He noted the picture of the chocolate sundae with the ice cream swimming in a pool of thick chocolate, smothered in whipped topping and crowned with a bright red cherry. Jamie's favorite.

He'd made light of discovering The Cookie Jar, claiming he *just happened* to be driving down Forty-third when he caught sight of it. That was all a lie.

He'd almost gone crazy when he hadn't heard from his sweet, adoring wife by Sunday and he'd gone out for a drive in an effort to collect his thoughts. Going past their old high school and his friends' favorite ice-cream parlor had been no accident. He would have gone inside then, but the café-style restaurant had been closed. He wasn't sure what had caused him to suggest the two of them meet there.

An impossibly young waitress arrived with a glass of water and a small green pad, ready to take his order. Rich chose a cheeseburger, a strawberry milk shake and an order of curly fries. The meal probably contained enough cholesterol to clog the Alaska pipeline, but what the hell. A stroll down memory lane was worth something.

Once his order was in, Rich decided to check out the songs on the jukebox. He was somewhat surprised to find he didn't recognize a single tune. Not even one. Surely the kids these days enjoyed golden oldies. His hands in his pockets fingered a few quarters, but after a couple of moments he decided to save his money and returned to the booth.

He was getting old. It hadn't impacted Rich before, but it did so now, sinking like a deadweight in the pit of his stomach. When the waitress didn't look any older than twelve and he didn't recognize a single Top 40 hit, then he'd best admit it—he was past his prime.

The cheeseburger was sinfully delicious. The French fries were just the way he liked them—hot and salty. He savored the sweet-tasting shake and couldn't remember a meal he'd enjoyed more.

Wrong.

It didn't do any good to try to fool himself. Any meal shared with Jamie would have suited him far better. Damn but he missed her. He missed their early-morning conversations and the sweet sound of her laughter. He missed the special talk they shared as they planned their child's future.

Their child.

Paul's three-year-old twin sons had been up and about for part of Saturday night, racing around the house in their Teenage Mutant Ninja Turtles pajamas.

For part of the evening, Jason had played cards while holding Ryan on his lap, while Rich held a squirming Ronnie. Rich had always enjoyed his young nephews, but he hadn't really appreciated the two until that evening. If all went well, within a year's time he'd be holding a son or daughter of his own. Knowing that had filled him with an electrified anticipation. He'd managed to keep those feelings in a holding pattern, not knowing what was happening between him and Jamie. But he would soon. They were going to clear the air.

When he'd first thought up the idea of marriage, Jamie had been afraid something like this would happen. She'd chatted endlessly with dire predictions, claiming sex between them would ruin everything.

To hear Jamie, she was utterly convinced that once they'd stepped over their self-imposed boundaries and indulged in the forbidden fruit, all would be lost, and they'd be banished from the gates of paradise. At the time he'd scoffed. He hadn't understood or appreciated her wisdom.

Now they were in danger of ruining everything, unless they dealt with their feelings on a mature, honest level. As for their lovemaking ruining their relationship, Rich wasn't sure he agreed. In some ways he felt their night together had probably saved their relationship. There was no telling how long they would have needlessly continued wearing blinders.

What a discovery they'd made. His smile grew cocky, then reality settled in.

What a mess he'd gotten them into.

He should never have made love to her, but try as he might, Rich couldn't make himself regret it. If he suffered any remorse it was that it took an argument for him to realize how much he cared for Jamie.

Talk about blind men! Rich had been in love with her for years, only he hadn't realized it. Men and women can go all their lives and never share the rare friendship they did. Rich didn't want to do or say anything that would jeopardize their marriage or their friendship.

Matters hadn't gone well when he'd phoned her Monday afternoon. The tension between them was taut enough to support a high-wire artist. Rich had said none of what he'd wanted to say, nor had he done anything to assure her of his love. Jamie had sounded stilted and uncertain. The conversation was over almost before it started. He'd been tempted to call her again several times since, but decided it would be best to wait until they could meet face-to-face. There was less likelihood of misunderstandings that way.

Rich had done a lot of thinking about what he intended to say to her. First they needed to clear the air, put aside any pettiness and discuss their feelings. It sounded good, and he sincerely hoped it worked. If everything went well, he'd go home with her and spend the night.

Why not?

They were married, for heaven's sake. It didn't make sense to create their child by artificial means when they were fully capable of doing it naturally.

Capable and eager.

He didn't plan to bring up their sleeping arrangement with her right away of course, but by heaven, he intended on letting her know it was what he wanted.

During the extra time spent waiting for her, Rich entertained several sensible ways of handling their discussion. Furthermore, he felt they should seriously consider moving in together. Since Jamie owned her place, it made sense for him to make the switch, but they'd eventually buy a house.

He was mulling over which neighborhood would be best for them when Jamie walked into The Cookie Jar. She wore a full-length navy blue coat with large white buttons.

"Hi. I'm not late, am I?" she asked, slipping into the seat opposite him.

Damn, but she looked good. Rich had trouble keeping his eyes off her. "No...no." He motioned for the waitress and ordered coffee.

"Me, too," Jamie said, smiling up at the teenager.

"You want to order your chocolate sundae now?"

She shook her head. "No thanks, I'm still recuperating from the flu." She folded her hands primly in her lap, her gaze avoiding his.

This didn't look as promising as Rich had hoped. "So you're still battling the bug?" Now that she mentioned it, she did look pale.

She nodded, her gaze following their waitress.

"They sure come young these days, don't they?" he said, his eyes following hers.

She glanced his way as though she didn't understand him. Rich motioned toward the teenager.

Jamie nodded, and a hint of a smile touched her eyes. "Pretty, too."

Rich hadn't noticed. A sixteen-year-old in braces and a training bra did little to excite him. Jamie on the other hand sent his senses into orbit. All he needed to do was play it cool, smile and reassure her as best he could, and if everything went well, he'd be in her bed that very night.

The girl delivered their coffee and smiled demurely at Jamie and Rich. Jamie returned her smile and reached

for the sugar container. Rich couldn't remember her
using sugar before, but now wasn't the time to mention
it.

"I wanted to talk about what happened Friday
night," he said, leaning forward. His hands cupped the
coffee, the hot brew warming his palms through the
thick ceramic mug.

"Why?"

"Well, because..." He sipped his coffee before answering. Her question caught him off guard and he
needed a few seconds to gather his thoughts. "It's
brought another dimension into our relationship."

"H-how do you feel about... our relationship having another dimension?" Once again she cast her gaze
around the room, looking everywhere but at him.

"I think it has the potential for being good," he answered, striving to sound just a tad indifferent. If he let
on to how crazy in love he was the first five seconds after her arrival, it might frighten her.

"The potential for being good," she repeated, her
voice so low he had to strain to hear her.

"Yes, unfortunately we weren't able to discuss it
Saturday morning." Rich watched as Jamie's upper
body went stiff. Apparently she had some problems
with him leaving and he'd best make his amends now.
"I apologize about heading out early. I realize it might
have..."

"Stop." She raised her hand and waved it side to side.
"Stop?"

"There's no need for you to apologize. None. Since
I've been home the last few days, I've had plenty of time
to think over the situation."

"I've given the matter some thought myself." Apparently Jamie had come to the same conclusions as he

had, which went a long way toward putting him at ease. He reached for his coffee and leaned back against the booth's thick red padding, reassured they were on the same wavelength.

"You were right."

Rich nodded. A man always loves to hear the truth.

"Having dinner with Floyd was an error in good judgment on my part, although it was completely innocent. After your experience with Pamela, I should have been able to identify and understand your feelings. As your friend . . . I should have been able to hear what you were really saying. If there's any blame to be placed over . . . over what happened between us, then I want you to know . . ."

"Blame," Rich repeated heatedly. The word cut through him like a freshly sharpened knife. The quickfire of his anger shot adrenaline into his veins.

"Yes, I just wanted you to know, I'm willing to accept the blame."

Hearing it a second time didn't improve his mood any. Rich set his coffee mug back on the Formica-topped table with enough force for the brew to slosh over the edges. "No one said anything about placing or accepting blame. If that's what you're here to do, then I suggest we end this discussion right now."

"I was just trying to—"

"Then don't."

Jamie's gaze fell to her coffee mug which was cradled between her hands. Rich could see from the even rise and fall of her shoulders how hard she was trying to avoid another argument.

Rich was too damn mad to make the effort. Blame. She wanted to allot blame for the most fantastic night of his life. Hers, too, but she was too damn proud to admit it.

Everything he'd hoped to accomplish—making this marriage real in every sense, moving in together, buying a home and creating a child—a son or daughter who'd be born from their love—seemed to disappear right before his eyes. He'd longed for this meeting to bridge the way for them to advance naturally from friends to lovers. Old married lovers.

"I've done it again," she whispered.

"Done what?"

"Angered you."

He knew it hadn't been her intention to offend him. From the bewildered look in her eyes, Rich was certain she didn't know what had set him off.

"Yes, I'm angry." He was damn mad and he intended for her to know it.

"It's happened already, hasn't it?" Her words were so low, Rich half expected her to break into tears. "We've killed the friendship."

"Not necessarily." Damn, but she looked pale, and here he was furious with her when all he wanted to do was to take her in his arms and make love to her.

"I knew this would happen," she said with an expressive sigh. "Marriage between us just isn't going to work. Our feelings for one another are all muddled...we hardly know how to act around each other anymore."

Rich sat silent and morose. What she said was true.

"What do you suggest?" he asked after a while.

"I...I don't know anymore. I thought I knew what I wanted, now I'm not so sure."

Rich didn't know, either. He wanted her for his wife, but he needed to be sure she shared his feelings. What man didn't need those types of reassurances? Damn, it had all sounded so simple earlier. Now he was floundering, confused and uncertain.

"Do you feel up to walking?" he asked.

His suggestion apparently caught Jamie by surprise. She nodded.

"Good." Rich reached for their tab, studied it, then left some money on the table.

They were in the old neighborhood now. The brick high school they'd once attended was two blocks over. By tacit agreement they headed in that direction. Jamie wrapped a scarf around her neck and buried her hands in her pockets. Rich also stuffed his hands into his pockets, but he'd have rather held hands with her.

They'd gone a block or so before either of them spoke.

"I always thought you were the handsomest boy in school."

"Me?" Rich laughed. "You certainly didn't let me know that."

"I couldn't. You were already vain."

Rich smiled. "I used to wish I had as easy a time with grades as you did."

"Easy?" she repeated with a short, mocking laugh. "I worked my tail off."

"Remember our ten-year reunion?"

Jamie nodded. "You were with some blonde. You always did like blondes, didn't you?"

"They're all right. You were with that guy who resembled Tommy Smothers."

"Ralph was a nice guy."

"Nice and dull." Rich didn't know why he'd bothered to bring Elaine. He'd much rather have spent the evening with Jamie. As it was, they'd danced nearly every dance together.

"At least all Ralph's brains weren't located below his neckline."

"Speaking of bustlines," Rich said, grinning boyishly.

Jamie whirled around to face him, her eyes spitting fire. "Don't you dare bring up the size of my bust. Don't... you dare."

Rich couldn't have held in a smile to save his soul. "You're full of surprises, aren't you?"

"Did I ever mention the karate lessons I took? I learned how to disarm a man in three easy moves. Don't tempt me, Manning."

"You tempt me." Rich didn't know what made him say it, but now that it was out, he wasn't sorry. Jamie went still at his side, her steps frozen in the dim light coming from the street lamp. Rich raised his hand and glided his fingertips over the soft shape of her face. Her eyes drifted shut.

"I... don't think this is a good idea...."

He stopped her, tracing the outline of her lips with his index finger. He circled once, twice, three times, each foray followed by her tongue, moistening her mouth.

"Why shouldn't I?"

Her eyes remained closed, and she swayed toward him. Rich reached for her, pressing her toward him. Her breasts met his chest and even through the thickness of two coats, he could feel how round and full they were.

"There... was something I wanted to say," she whispered.

"Oh." He buried his face in her sweet-smelling hair, drinking in her softness, her gentleness. Rich didn't know how it happened, how they could ever be at odds with one another when the loving was this good.

"You . . . you shouldn't distract me."

"Do you want me to stop?" His lips grazed the underside of her jaw. She rotated her head and sighed softly.

"Not yet. . . ."

"Should I kiss you?"

"Please."

It was all the encouragement he needed. He slanted his mouth over hers and wrapped his arms around her so securely he nearly lifted her from the sidewalk. Her arms crept up his chest, pausing at his shoulders. The kissing was even better than it had been before, something Rich hadn't thought was possible.

His mouth moved hungrily over hers, and when she sighed and parted her lips, he swept her mouth with his tongue. Jamie reacted with a swift intake of breath and wound her arms around his neck.

Rich had never intended on kissing her like this. Not on a public street half a block from where they'd attended high school. He wanted her soft and yielding in his arms. But he needed her home and in his bed. And soon.

The taste of salty moistness caught him by storm. She was crying. He pulled his mouth from hers. "Jamie, what's wrong?"

"Everything . . . nothing." She kissed him back, her need great, her open mouth pressing over his. It was as lusty as anything he'd ever known.

"You're crying."

"I know."

"Why?"

"Because you're making everything so difficult."

"How am I doing that?" She remained in his embrace, with his hand pressing at the small of her back.

"Kissing me . . . You weren't supposed to do that."

"I'm not?"

"No . . . but don't stop."

"I don't intend to." Rich didn't need further encouragement. His kiss was urgent, filled with unleashed desire. Damn if they weren't both the biggest fools he'd ever known. They'd wasted precious days, hiding behind their fears. All along they could have been sharing the discovery of their love.

"Rich . . ."

Reluctantly, he broke off the kiss, his chest heaving with the effort it took to break away from her. His heart was roaring like a jet engine. He reached for her hand, tucking it in his own, and headed back toward The Cookie Jar. "Let's get out of here."

"I . . . suppose we should."

"It's either that or have me make love to you in the middle of the street."

"Make love to me?"

Surely it was what she expected. A man didn't kiss a woman like that without her knowing what he had in mind, especially if that woman was his wife!

"But . . . we need to talk."

"Later." His steps were brisk. The sooner he arrived at his apartment, the sooner he could kiss her again. He didn't want to give her the opportunity to change her mind.

"There's something we should talk over first."

"First?" The woman had no conception of the frustration she was forcing him to endure.

"I would have said it earlier.... I planned to, but then you suggested the walk and... we started kissing and now I'm more confused than ever."

He stopped at his car, unlocked the passenger door then turned to face her. Resting his hands on her shoulders, he met her gaze and was relieved to note how hungry her eyes were. "All right, Jamie, say whatever it is you want and be done with it."

She brushed the moisture from her cheeks, then drew in a deep, steadying breath. "In light of Friday night."

That again! "Yes?"

"I was thinking you might want to... you know?"

Rich had an inkling. She was about to suggest what he'd been giving serious thought to for the last several days, that they take this marriage seriously and move in together.

"If it's what you want, it's what I want," he said, brushing the hair from her face, his fingers lingering against the silky softness of her skin.

Her eyes squeezed closed, and she bit into her trembling lower lip. "I don't know what I want anymore... and I don't think you do, either."

"Sure I do," he countered. He wanted her.

"I think we should give serious consideration to..."

"To what?"

Her lips trembled, and she lowered her gaze. "A divorce."

Chapter Nine

Rich jerked away from her as though he'd received an electric shock.

"A divorce!" he bellowed.

It wasn't the alternative Jamie preferred, but she felt honor-bound to offer Rich the option. They'd broken their agreement, the promises they'd made to each other before the wedding ceremony.

The decision to make love had been mutual, nevertheless everything had changed, and they couldn't continue pretending it hadn't. Their lovemaking was so beautiful, it had felt spiritual. Jamie would treasure the memory of their night together all her life. Every time she thought about falling asleep with her head nestled over Rich's heart, she went weak.

"A divorce," Rich repeated.

Jamie shuddered. He would never know what it had cost her to make the offer. With all her being, Jamie prayed Rich would give her some indication that Friday night had been as meaningful and as beautiful for him as it had been for her.

"So you want a divorce?" he said, slamming closed the passenger door to his car. The sound vibrated like a shotgun into the stillness of the night.

"I . . . I didn't say it was what I wanted."

"Then why did you suggest it?"

"Because . . . well, because matters are different between us now."

"You're damn right they're different. I don't even know you anymore."

Jamie chose to ignore his outburst. "We'd agreed this was to be a marriage of convenience."

"You didn't exactly fight me off, you know."

Jamie's cheeks exploded with scalding color. "No . . . I didn't, but it doesn't alter the fact we broke our arrangement . . . and before we go on with our plans, I feel we should reevaluate our options and our commitment."

"You sound just like a banker. Cold and calculating. What's the matter? Are you afraid of a little emotion?" His eyes were seething with anger.

Jamie thought he was furious when he'd confronted her with Floyd, but his anger of Friday night paled in comparison to the fury she saw now.

"We're not teenagers anymore," she stated as calmly as her voice would allow. "Hopefully we're responsible, mature adults who can make decisions based on something other than hormones."

"So Friday night was nothing more than a tumble in the hay for you?"

"I didn't say that," Jamie argued, growing angry herself. "You're purposely misconstruing everything

I'm trying to explain. Friday night happened ... good or bad, it happened. We can't go on pretending it didn't."

"I had no intention of forgetting it or ignoring it or anything else you claim."

"Then why did it take you until Monday afternoon to contact me?" she cried, firing questions. "Why did you sneak away in the middle of the night without a word? I woke up feeling like a one-night stand."

"You aren't the only one disappointed," Rich barked. "It wouldn't have hurt you any to contact me."

"You abandoned me," she accused.

"I made you feel like a one-night stand?" Rich paced the sidewalk along the side of his car, his steps clipped. He rammed his fingers forcefully through his hair. "A one-night stand? That's ridiculous. For heaven's sake, we're married."

"We're not," she argued heatedly. "Not really. I don't ..."

"I've got the papers to prove it. Talk about denial! A wedding is a wedding, so don't try to add a list of qualifiers to it now."

"Those qualifiers were added *before* the ceremony."

"So you want out." He turned toward her, his face contorted with anger, his blue eyes piercing and intense.

"It wouldn't be fair to tell you what I want.... I'm giving you the option. Our relationship has changed, and we can't pretend it hasn't."

"And I am?"

"Yes!" she shouted. "If I hadn't said anything we'd be halfway to your place by now. We both know I would have ended up spending the night, and then what?"

She didn't give him the opportunity to answer. She knew what would have happened. They both knew.

"Then tomorrow morning," she continued, "everything would be awkward again and there wouldn't be time to do or say much of anything because we both need to get to work."

Already Jamie could picture the scene in her mind. They'd be rushing around dressing, embarrassed and uncomfortable with one another, the way they'd been when Rich had phoned her Monday afternoon. There wouldn't be time to talk, but they would exchange polite pleasantries while he drove her back to Forty-third street so she could pick up her car. Then she'd have to dash home and change clothes again before heading for the bank.

"It wouldn't need to be that way."

"But it would have been." After a few kisses neither one of them would have wanted to talk, not when they were so eager for the loving.

"What I don't understand is why you're throwing a divorce in my face now."

It all made logical sense to Jamie. "We were planning a divorce anyway, after the baby's born. There were stipulations, agreements we made long before the wedding. That's all changed. If you're going to experience second thoughts, the time is now."

"Is it me or you who's experiencing regrets?" he demanded harshly.

"We weren't discussing me."

"Maybe we should be."

"Oh, Rich, please don't."

"Don't what?"

"Try to turn everything I say around. I didn't mean to offend or hurt you. I just want this to be as clear as we can make it. Creating a child is too important a decision to get muddled up in egos."

"It's even more difficult when it's my ego you keep knifing."

"I'm not doing it intentionally. All I want is for us to be honest with each other. If you decide you'd rather forget the whole thing, then I'll understand. Good heavens, look what's happened thus far! We've nearly destroyed the marriage and we haven't been married six weeks. This isn't going to be quite as simple as we thought."

Rich rubbed his hand down his face, looking confused.

A divorce wasn't what Jamie wanted, but she felt in all fairness she had to offer him the opportunity to end their plans now before their relationship was complicated further with a child.

"I was so confident before."

"I . . . was, too." Jamie could barely stand the suspense, but she couldn't say or do anything to encourage him one way or the other. They both had to be utterly confident that they were doing the right thing. "Would you prefer to take a couple of days to think it over?"

Rich's gaze found hers. "Maybe I should. I thought I knew, but maybe I don't."

Disappointed, Jamie nodded. "I'll wait to hear from you then." She secured the purse strap over her shoulder and offered him a smile. A weak smile. "Good night, then."

"'Night."

She headed toward her car, which was parked four or five spaces down from his own. Her heart was in her throat, and she struggled not to reveal any of what she was feeling. Rich surprised her by walking the short distance with her.

"I've really made a mess of this, haven't I?" he asked. For the first time since she mentioned the divorce, he didn't look as though he wanted to bite her head off.

"We both have," she answered in a small voice. She tried to smile up at him and failed. She paused when she reached her car and opened her purse, searching for her keys.

"I don't know if it makes any difference," Rich said, and his eyes burned into hers, "but I'd like you to know I had to work Saturday morning. I probably should have woken you. I assumed my singing in the shower would have, but when it didn't, I decided to let you sleep. It was thoughtless of me not to leave a note."

"You were at work?" Although he'd explained it to her, Jamie had to say it herself in order to absorb it.

Rich nodded. "When I did phone, you weren't there."

"But there wasn't a message on my machine."

He shrugged. "After what I went through Friday, I was through talking to that machine of yours. You might have phoned me." The last bit was made as an offhanded suggestion, but it did little to disguise his disappointment in her.

"I did...but you weren't home. I didn't leave a message, either." What a fool she'd been. What fools they'd both been. Jamie wanted to groan at their stupidity.

"You phoned?" His sigh of frustration was audible.

"You did, too?" Her sigh joined his.

Jamie resisted the urge to weep. There'd been so much she'd wanted to say, and hadn't. So much she'd longed to tell him. And couldn't. The loving between them had been perfect. Jamie couldn't remember anything ever being that good.

"You'll phone me...soon?" she asked, disguising how anxious she was to hear from him.

Rich nodded, then lifted one corner of his mouth in a half smile. "I'll leave a message on your machine if you're not in this time."

"If you don't phone me, then I'm calling you." She wasn't willing to leave room for any additional misunderstandings. Not again. Never again, she vowed.

Before he realized where he was heading, Rich found himself at Jason's apartment complex. He sat for several minutes in the parking lot, mulling over his thoughts.

When Jamie first mentioned a divorce, he thought he'd explode. Rich couldn't remember being more angry in his life. Angry and hurt and confused. They were minutes away from making love, and she batted the word at him as though she were talking about Sunday dinner with her mother.

Divorce.

The woman was a fruitcake. At one time he had accepted there was no reasoning with her, and the best thing to do was walk away from the whole mess, then the unexpected happened.

She'd started to make sense.

Jamie always had been the logical one. The perfectionist. Everything had to be just right. It had driven him to distraction when they were on the yearbook staff together. He should have realized that although thirteen years had passed since they'd graduated from high school, Jamie hadn't changed.

She wanted everything as clear as they could make it. Those were her words.

Rich knew what he wanted, too. He wanted her back in his bed so he could make love to her again. Naturally he didn't say as much. How could he? She was spouting off about them denying what happened, claiming they couldn't go on pretending nothing had changed when everything was different. Rich didn't know how she could think any of those things when he was doing his damnedest to get her back into his bed.

Hours later, Rich still didn't know what to make of their meeting. He needed a sounding board, and so he'd elected Jason, whether his older brother was willing or not.

The lights were out in Jason's apartment, but that didn't deter Rich any. He leaned on the buzzer until a sliver of light shot out from under the door.

He waited until he heard the lock open, then stepped back.

"Rich?" His brother groaned, tying the knot in his bathrobe. "What the hell are you doing here this time of night?"

Rich checked his watch and was surprised to discover it was after eleven. He'd been sitting and thinking for longer than he'd realized.

"I need to talk," he said, marching past Jason and into the kitchen.

A yawning Jason followed closely behind. "Is this going to take long?"

"I don't know, why? Have you got a woman with you?"

"If I had, I wouldn't have answered the door no matter how long you leaned on the doorbell." Jason pulled out a kitchen chair, sat down and slouched for-

ward over his folded arms. "In case you haven't noticed, I'm not in the talking mood."

"Don't worry, all I need you to do is listen."

Rich walked over to the refrigerator and opened it.
He brought out two cold sodas and pushed one toward
his brother. "When was the last time you bought groceries?"

"I don't know. Why?"

"All you've got in there is a tin can with a fork stick-
ing out of it."

"Dinner," Jason said, covering his mouth with a
yawn. He waited a moment, then gestured with his
hand. "Go on . . . talk. I'm listening."

Now that he had the floor, so to speak, Rich wasn't
sure where to start. He wasn't ashamed of having made
love to Jamie, but he wasn't sure how she would feel if
she knew he was talking to Jason about their night together.

"You need some help, little brother?" Jason asked,
straightening and opening his soda.

"No," Rich denied vehemently.

"I'll give it to you anyway. You and Jamie have suc-
cumbed to the delights of the flesh and now you don't
know what to do about it."

Rich was so flabbergasted that all he could do was
stare at his brother, his mouth open wide. He snapped
it closed when he realized what he was doing.

Jason ignored him and guzzled half the can of soda
in three giant gulps.

"How'd you figure that out?"

"I knew Saturday night," Jason informed him, wip-
ing off his mouth with the back of his hand. "A blind
man could have figured it out."

"How . . . what did I say?"

"Nothing. I asked you if Jamie was pregnant yet, remember?"

Rich wasn't likely to forget. The question had hit him like a sledgehammer. Jason's inquisitiveness was what led Rich to contact her Monday afternoon. Jamie might well be pregnant from their one night together, although she'd been quick to reassure him otherwise.

"So?" Rich asked, feigning ignorance.

"A shocked look came over you and you closed up tighter than a razor clam. It was obvious, at least to me, there was a possibility she might well be 'with child.'"

"It's not that simple."

"Women and marriage rarely are. Why do you think I've avoided it all these years? I tried to tell you before the wedding, but would you listen? Ah, no, this was different you said. You and Jamie were friends entering into a business agreement. Nothing more and nothing less."

"I remember what I said," Rich muttered, taking another swallow of his pop. He wasn't so thirsty as he was frustrated. He'd been incredibly naive when it came to this marriage business. Hell, the whole thing had sounded like a great idea; it still did.

"What's the matter now?"

Rich crushed the empty aluminum pop can between his hands. "I just met with Jamie for the first time since . . . since I spent the night."

"It didn't go well."

Rich shrugged. "Let's put it this way. She suggested a divorce."

"A divorce? Good grief, Rich, what did you say to the poor girl?"

Rich found it interesting that Jason would place the blame on him. "The hell if I know. She came up with the idea all on her own. The way she figures it, I . . . we changed the rules and according to Jamie, we need to step back and reevaluate our commitment.''

Jason leaned back in his chair, its two front legs lifting up from the floor. ''Sounds serious. Are you looking at a reevaluation?''

''Yeah,'' Rich said forcefully. ''I think we should throw the whole prenuptial agreement out the window and move in together.''

''In other words, you want this to be a real marriage?''

''Yes. Hell, yes.''

''But you don't think Jamie would be willing to go for that?''

''I don't know.'' He'd like to think she would, but he'd suffered more than one setback lately when it came to reading a woman's mind. He wasn't nearly as confident as he had been earlier.

''So what are you going to do?''

''I wish I knew.''

''Do you love her?''

Rich nodded without hesitation. ''Like crazy.'' Standing, he walked over to the sink and leaned against the counter, crossing his arms. ''No one is more surprised than I am. I didn't have a clue that I felt anything more than friendship for Jamie. I didn't even notice how really beautiful she is until recently.''

''What do you intend to do about it?''

''If I knew that, I wouldn't be pounding down your door in the middle of the night.'' Rich's response was short-tempered, but Jason should have been able to figure that much out for himself.

"Good point." Jason rubbed his hand across the lower half of his face. "I don't suppose sleeping on it makes much sense right now."

"If there were any possibility I could sleep, I'd be home in bed." Rich had lived alone for years, but the thought of returning to an empty apartment filled him with dread. He wanted to be with Jamie. It didn't even matter if they made love or not; he needed her. Needed her reassurances. Needed her warmth, her laughter. Needed her love.

"I wish I knew what she wanted," he muttered.

"Who?"

Rich tossed his brother a scathing look. "Jamie, who else?"

"There's no need to bite my head off."

"Then don't ask stupid questions."

Jason yawned loudly, meaningfully, but Rich ignored his brother's broad hint. "She didn't give me a single indication of how she felt. Absolutely nothing."

"At the expense of appearing stupid," Jason muttered mournfully, "an indication about what?"

"The divorce." Rich couldn't remember his brother being so obtuse. "She offered it to me as an option, but when I asked what she wanted, she wouldn't say."

"She couldn't."

"Why not?"

"Because," Jason responded between yawns, "you'd be influenced by what she said and she wants the decision to be yours. She's a smart gal."

Rich paced the compact kitchen. "I told her I'd think everything over and get back to her."

"Then go home and sleep on it," Jason said, standing. He ushered Rich toward the front door. "In case you haven't noticed, I'm not exactly at my brightest, and I've got surgeries scheduled all day tomorrow.''

Rich brushed off his coat sleeves and chuckled. ''I can take a hint.''

Jason grinned and slowly shook his head. ''No, you can't.''

''This is Dr. Fullerton's office.''

''Hello,'' Jamie said, her hand tightening around the telephone receiver. ''I...need to cancel my appointment with Dr. Fullerton.'' She listed the date and time for the receptionist.

''Would you like to reschedule now?''

Jamie would have liked nothing better, but not knowing what Rich would decide made the effort futile. ''Not now, thank you. I'll give you a call the first part of next week.''

Jamie had delayed contacting Dr. Fullerton's office all day. She'd hoped to hear from Rich right away. Dreamer that she was. In her optimistic imagination, she had him phoning first thing in the morning with the assurances that he felt as strongly committed to their marriage and their child as ever.

When she hadn't heard from him by noon, she had no other option but to cancel her appointment. It wasn't the end of the world. Yet she struggled with her emotions for the remainder of the afternoon.

She knew she was in trouble when she tossed a frozen entrée into her microwave for dinner and munched on miniature-size marshmallows while watching a re-run of *Love Connection*. So much for good eating habits or any semblance of healthy emotions. She'd sunk about as far as she'd ever gone.

Jamie, who was normally so meticulous about her clothes, didn't bother to change after work. Instead, she traipsed around the condo in her business suit, her blouse pulled from her waist. Her slippers made shuffling noises as she migrated from one room to the next with no real purpose or direction. She'd have liked to blame her lethargy on her recent bout with the flu, but she knew otherwise.

What was really troubling her was her husband. Or rather, her lack of a real one. In their discussion the night before, she'd tried to be as forthright and honest with Rich as she could. She hadn't hinted at her feelings one way or the other. Now she wasn't so sure she'd made the right decision. She might have mentioned, even casually, how much Rich's willingness to follow through with their agreement meant to her. Perhaps if she'd reassured him of how good a mother she planned to be, their evening might have turned out differently.

No. That would have been emotional blackmail.

She couldn't have said any of those things any more than she could have admitted how much she loved him. Or how eager she was for them to explore the budding love between them.

Jamie was pacing in front of the television, holding on to the plastic bag of marshmallows and mulling over her troubled thoughts when the doorbell chimed.

Her heart lurched. It could be Rich, but she knew better than to hope. Far more likely it was her neighbor telling her the television was too loud.

Her mouth was full of marshmallows, which she attempted to hurriedly swallow. It didn't work, although she was chewing as fast as she could. She unlocked the door and nearly choked when Rich smiled boldly in her direction.

"Hi."

She raised her right hand, as though she were making a pledge.

"There's something wrong with your cheeks. Have you got the mumps?"

She wildly shook her head, chewed some more and swallowed a mouthful of marshmallows whole. "Hi," she said, her heart doing giant leapfrogs against her rib cage. "I . . . I wasn't expecting you."

"I know. Rather than take a chance with that answering machine of yours, I decided to stop over. You don't mind, do you?"

"Of course I don't mind." If he had so much as an inkling of how pleased she was to see him, he'd be really smiling instead of grinning at her with those huge blue eyes of his. She knew she was staring, but Jamie couldn't stop looking at Rich. It was almost as if she weren't completely sure he was really there.

"Something doesn't smell right," he said, wrinkling his nose and sniffing the air. He followed the scent into her kitchen, walked over to the microwave and opened the door. He cringed and waved his hand in front of the now-cooked entrée.

"My dinner," she explained, stuffing the bag of marshmallows into the silverware drawer.

"I thought you'd given up on this stuff."

"I had . . . but I wasn't in the mood to cook tonight."

"Why not?"

"Because I had to cancel my appointment with Dr. Fullerton and I was depressed. I know I'm depressed when I crave marshmallows and turn on *Love Connection*. Life doesn't get any bleaker than that."

Rich was looking at her as though he'd never seen her before.

"Go ahead and make fun of me."

"I wouldn't dream of it."

"Sure you would." She swiped the back of her hand under her nose, realizing she'd probably never looked more pitiful in her life. "I'll have you know I didn't get into the marshmallows when I broke up with Tony."

"In other words I'm responsible for reducing you to this level?"

"Not exactly. I can't blame everything on you. Let's just say you're responsible for my watching *Love Connection*."

Rich grinned and brushed a stray strand of hair from her temple, his fingers lingering there. "Would it help any if I told you I've come to a decision?"

"Probably." She was almost afraid to hope what it would be.

Instead of telling her what he'd decided, he removed her dinner from the microwave, carried it over to the garbage can and tossed it inside.

"If you want junk food, we'll order pizza, all right?"

She nodded eagerly. The *we* part didn't escape her notice. Apparently he intended on staying awhile, which was fine with her. More than fine.

"While we're at it, I think it would be best if you ditched the marshmallows, too."

"All right." She jerked open her silverware drawer and handed him her stash.

"One more thing."

"Yes?" She gazed up at him, her heart in her eyes. She tried not to let her feelings show but it was impossible.

"Why did you cancel the appointment with Dr. Fullerton?"

"Because...you know." She rubbed the palms of her hands together. "I didn't hear from you this morning...not that I expected I would, I mean, overnight was much too soon for you to have made up your mind. It would have been unreasonable for me to expect anything of the sort." Jamie knew she was rambling, but she couldn't seem to make herself stop. "My...our appointment with Dr. Fullerton is...was for tomorrow and I couldn't very well go through the insemination process, could I?"

"You've already been through one insemination process." He seemed to take delight in reminding her of that.

"Yes, I know, but...this was different."

His mouth slanted upward, his eyes bright with laughter. "I should hope so."

"I didn't want to cancel the appointment." It probably wasn't fair to say so, not if he hadn't made his decision.

"Any chance you can reschedule?"

"Ah..." Her gaze connected with his, her heart pounding as loud as an African drum. "Are you saying, you've decided you want to stay married and to have the baby and—"

"That's exactly what I want."

Jamie couldn't help herself. She let out a cry of sheer joy, threw her arms around his neck and brought his mouth down to hers.

Chapter Ten

A moan of surprise and welcome escaped Rich as Jamie's mouth sought out his. He wrapped his arms around her as she stepped deeper into his embrace. His breath, her breath, came heavy and abrupt as if they'd both been caught off guard by the power of their attraction. The power of their need.

Rich tried to discipline his response to her soft, feminine body, but his arousal was fierce and sudden, too sudden for him to tame.

Rich wanted Jamie as he'd never wanted anyone. He needed her. The kiss, which had began as a spontaneous reaction of joy and excitement, quickly became a carnal feast of desperation and desire.

Rich groaned. He couldn't stop himself. His wife was in his arms, where she belonged, where he intended to keep her. He plunged his tongue hungrily into her mouth, and his hands roved down the gentle curve of her spine, over the firm cheeks of her buttocks. He lifted her intimately upward, pressing her against the solid heat of his arousal.

Jamie moaned and rotated the lower half of her body against him. Sweet heaven, he was hard. Their kissing continued, Rich sipping at her lips, drinking of her sweetness, her excitement. The longing to make love to her, to join their bodies as God intended, was almost unbearable. He battled the urge, promising himself the time would come soon enough when he could have her again.

Patience, patience his mind chanted. They'd make love soon, very soon and when they did, it would be a celebration of their love and their marriage. There would be no grounds for regrets or misgivings. No room for doubts. It would all come in time. *Soon,* Rich promised himself. *Soon.*

By a supreme act of his will, Rich drew in a tattered, shaky breath and buried his face in her hair. "You taste of marshmallows."

"I'm sorry."

"Don't be." It demanded more control than he'd ever imagined he'd need to ease himself from her arms. "What about ordering that pizza?"

"Sure." She recovered quickly, Rich noted. Far more quickly than he did. She brushed the hair from her face and smiled shakily up at him. "Tuesday's mail had a coupon as I recall.... I'll check to be sure."

"Pepperoni and sausage?"

"Sounds good to me," she agreed over her shoulder. She moved away from him as if they'd never touched. Rich envied her ability to do so. He had difficulty disguising her effect on him and even more trouble walking normally.

Jamie pulled out a kitchen drawer where she maintained a small file for coupons. Once again he was amazed at how organized she was. Within a couple of minutes, she'd located what she wanted and had placed the order.

The pizza arrived thirty prompt minutes later and by then they were back on an even keel with one another. Rich would have liked to discuss the kiss, but didn't want to say or do anything to destroy this fragile, new-found peace. There would be plenty of time later for them to talk about their feelings. For now, he would bask in the warm glow of his love and wait patiently for Jamie to learn to love him back.

It shouldn't take long. He didn't mean to be cocky about his attractiveness or charm, but their love would be built on the firm foundation of friendship. All he had to do was exhibit patience and tenderness. The way he figured, it shouldn't take more than a week or two. By then he'd be confident enough to approach her with the truth of his love. By the end of the month he'd be moving in with her.

No one would fault his plan. Least of all Jamie. He'd bide his time, give her the love and attention she needed, prove that he could be a good husband to her, as good a husband as he intended being a father to their child.

If everything went according to his plans, Jamie would be pregnant long before they could follow through with their appointment with Dr. Fullerton.

Soon the pizza box lay open on the kitchen table. Jamie had set out plates and napkins and two cold cans of pop.

"This tastes good."

Rich agreed with a nod of his head. The pizza was excellent, but it couldn't compare in taste to Jamie's sweet kisses. If he wasn't careful, he could easily become addicted to the flavor that was hers alone.

"I'll contact Dr. Fullerton's office in the morning," she announced casually. "I probably won't be able to get in until next month." Her gaze briefly met his, as though she was seeking his approval.

"That sounds fine to me."

Her dark eyes brightened and her hand reached for his. "We're gong to make this work. We can, I know it."

"Of course we can," Rich agreed. If everything went according to plan, they'd soon be a family and that was exactly the way Rich intended them to stay. Jamie didn't know that yet, but she'd discover his intentions before long, and by that time she'd be as eager as he was.

The alarm sounded and Jamie rolled onto her back, swung out her arm and flipped off the buzzer. The irritating beep was replaced with the gentle sounds of the soft rock-music station she habitually listened to each morning.

The bed was warm and cozy and she didn't relish the thought of crawling out into the dark, cold world, especially on a Monday morning. It was far more pleasant to linger beneath a thick layer of blankets and think about the good things that were happening between her and Rich.

They hadn't seen a good deal of each other in the past week because Rich was deeply involved in a defense project for Boeing. He'd worked three to four hours overtime every night plus both days of the weekend. Yet he consistently took time each day to contact her.

He sounded so frustrated at not seeing her as often as he wanted. As often as she wanted. Jamie had done her best to pretend it didn't matter, but it did. She missed him dreadfully, although their late-night telephone conversations went a long way toward making up for that.

They were like a pair of teenagers talking on the phone. There wasn't all that much to discuss, yet they often spent an hour or more chatting away like magpies as if it had been weeks since they'd last spoken. Afterward, Jamie would spend the remainder of the night swaddled in happiness.

Rich was exhausted by the time he called her each night. Although he'd never said as much, she had the impression he raced out of the office and hurried home just so he could talk to her. It was what she wanted to think, Jamie supposed.

Although they hadn't been able to see much of each other, Jamie felt greatly encouraged by the way matters were developing between them. They were close, closer than they'd been at any time since high school. It seemed natural to have her life so closely entwined with his. Natural and right.

Everything was going so well for them. Rich seemed pleased when she rescheduled her appointment with Dr. Fullerton. Jamie often fantasized about their child. All along she'd hoped for a girl, and admitted as much. Rich had made his wishes known, too. He wanted a son. Although they'd only agreed to one baby, if everything went well, Jamie wouldn't be opposed to bearing a second child.

Stretching her arms high above her head, she yawned loudly and kicked herself free from her covers. Although she would prefer to laze the morning away thinking about Rich and their future, she had to shower and get ready for work.

Still yawning, she sat up and turned on the bedside lamp. The room started to sway. Not understanding what was happening, Jamie exhaled slowly and closed her eyes. The sensation worsened until she was forced to press her head back to her pillow. The dizziness was followed by a bout of nausea.

Apparently she was suffering from a relapse of the flu.

Jason contacted Rich at the office early Tuesday morning. "I haven't heard from you in a while," he gave as an excuse for the call. "I thought I'd check in to see how everything's coming along with you and Jamie."

"Fine," Rich said, stretching a design layout across the top of his desk. He pressed the phone to his ear with his shoulder as he worked. "I appreciated your words of wisdom the other night." However, as Rich recalled, Jason seemed more concerned about getting him out of his apartment than shedding any new light on Rich's muddled marriage.

Rich had been more shaken that night than he realized. The mere mention of the word *divorce* had disconcerted him. It had forced him to deal with the depth of his love for Jamie and had set his determination to do everything within his power to make their marriage work.

"So matters between you and Jamie are better?"

"So far, so good."

"No more talk of a divorce?"

"None." Thank God, Rich mused.

"Then you've agreed to her terms?"

"More or less." It was the terms they'd both agreed upon, only he wanted to change the rules now. All he needed was a few days free to convince Jamie how crazy she was about him. It shouldn't be that difficult, especially when he was so much in love with her.

"What does 'more or less' mean?" Jason wanted to know.

"It means," Rich said, his words heavy with impatience, "I intend on making this marriage real." He glanced around to be certain no one in the office across the hall from him could hear. This wasn't the way he intended his fellow workers to learn he was a married man.

"How does Jamie feel about this, or—" Jason hesitated, "—does she know?"

"She will soon enough." Rich had never felt more frustrated in his life. Just when matters were going along smoothly, this defense project had kicked in and he was swamped to the gills. Knowing that he'd volunteered for this project didn't improve his disposition any. He'd been single at the time, but matters had changed and he was a married man. Sort of a married man. Longing to be a husband to his wife.

"I don't suppose you've considered telling Mom and Dad you're married, have you?"

Jason should have taken up interrogation, Rich mused. He certainly possessed the skills.

"It wouldn't hurt, you know," Jason added.

Rich frowned. "Is there any reason I should tell them?"

The sound of Jason's chuckle flowed smoothly over the telephone wire. "Not really. Just promise me you'll let me be there when you do."

Rich didn't find any humor in his brother's teasing. "I will when the time's right." That might take longer than he'd originally planned, no thanks to all the overtime he'd been putting in lately. Informing his parents that he and Jamie were married and had been for the past six weeks wasn't a task he relished.

"I'll talk to you later."

"Right," Rich said absently, more concerned about the designs he was reviewing than the conversation with his older brother. He hung up the phone and checked his watch. If the day progressed as he'd planned, he'd have time to stop off and visit Jamie on his way home. Just for a few minutes. Just long enough to hold her and tell her how much he missed not being with her. Just enough to see him through the next four or five days until he could be with her again.

Rich was so involved in the designs that he didn't notice someone was standing in the doorway to his office until he happened to glance up. When he did, his eyes rounded with surprise.

"Jamie." Her own eyes were red and glazed with tears. Yet she was smiling as though she had the world by the tail. Rich didn't know which emotion to respond to first. "What's wrong?"

"Absolutely nothing," she cried, and raced toward him, arms outstretched. "Oh, Rich, you won't believe what's happened. You just won't believe it. I...I know I shouldn't have come here, not when you're so busy, but I had to, I simply had to."

Thinking she might have something seriously wrong with her, Rich scooted out his chair and had her sit down. Then he crouched in front of her, gripping the armrests of the chair, forming a protective barricade around her.

"Tell me," he said tenderly.

"I woke up sick yesterday," she muttered, opening her purse and digging through it for a tissue. When she located one, she dabbed it at the corners of her eyes. Once again she was smiling broadly yet weeping. Tears rolled down the sides of her face, and the edges of her mouth trembled with some undetermined emotion.

"I assumed I was having a relapse of the flu," she said, sobbing, "but I felt fine a little bit later. I didn't even think to mention it when you phoned last night...but this morning my stomach was queasy again and I felt light-headed—as though I was going to faint. I wasn't sure what to think until I checked the calendar."

"The calendar?"

She nodded enthusiastically.

"Jamie?" Rich was afraid to put too much connotation on what she was saying. She couldn't possibly mean what he thought. It was ludicrous. They'd only made love the one time.

Once again she nodded wildly. "Rich," she said, her hands gripping hold of his. "We're pregnant."

"Pregnant," Rich repeated in a whisper, stunned. If he hadn't been holding on to the sides of the chair, he was convinced he'd have toppled onto his backside. "Pregnant," he repeated slowly.

"I never dreamed it would happen so quickly. My temperature was only elevated a little that night and...I didn't really think I was in my fertile time yet, but obviously I was. Rich, oh, Rich," she sobbed joyfully, and covered her mouth with the tips of her fingers. "We're going to have a baby."

"A baby." Rich was caught completely by surprise. "You're sure? You've been to see Dr. Fullerton already?"

"No...there are these little tests. I bought one in the drugstore this morning first thing and it took just a few minutes and—"

"You're sure?"

"The stick turned blue. You can't get any more positive than that."

"Blue...does that mean the baby's a boy?" His head, his heart were racing at the speed of light, trying to take it all in.

Jamie laughed and hiccuped and laughed some more. "No, silly, it doesn't mean we're having a son, it means we're going to be parents."

"But we could very well be having a son," he challenged.

"Or daughter." She looped her arms around his neck and laughed, a free-flowing outpouring of her joy. The sound of it echoed against the walls of his office; it was the sweetest, most poignant song he'd ever heard.

"We're pregnant," Rich said, finally assimilating what she was saying. "We're really pregnant?"

"Really," she said, brushing the tips of her fingers over his face. "That's what I've been trying to tell you."

"Pregnant." Wrapping his arms around her waist, he stood, taking her with him. His mouth found hers, and he kissed her then the way he'd longed to do all week. Thoroughly, wholly, not leaving any portion of her mouth unexplored.

Jamie moaned. So did Rich. The kiss created a need for much more, and this was neither the time nor the place.

"Say something," she whispered, her eyes holding his captive. Her hands were pressing against the sides of his jaw. "Tell me you're pleased about the baby."

Everything he longed to tell her, his joy, his excitement, the overwhelming sense of love he experienced for her, all formed a huge lump in his throat. To his dismay, Rich couldn't utter a single word. Finally he threw back his head and released a shout that sounded something like a war cry.

"Rich?" Bill Hastings, a concerned frown pleating his brow, appeared in the doorway.

Rich grinned and waved. He broke away from Jamie, but kept her hand linked with his. "Hello, Bill. Have you met Jamie Manning, my wife?"

Jamie's gaze turned to his, and her smile grew and grew. "Jamie Warren Manning," she corrected.

"Your wife?" Bill frowned, but recovered quickly. "When did this happen? You never said a word. This isn't the same Jamie Warren you . . . you know."

"Yup," Jamie answered for him. "I'm the one he wanted you to date."

"You two are married?"

"We'd better be." Rich said, tucking his arm around Jamie's slim waist. The time would come when that same waist would be filled with his child. He went all mushy inside thinking about it. Rich didn't realize men were susceptible to those kinds of emotions. He assumed they were reserved exclusively for women. His heart felt full. Overflowing with a joy so profound, he'd never thought to experience anything like it. His throat thickened as though it wouldn't take much for him to break into tears. Rich couldn't remember the last time he'd wept. It wasn't something a man did often. But knowing his child, his son or daughter, was growing beneath Jamie's heart was enough to reduce him to tears.

"I see," Bill said slowly, clearly not comprehending a thing.

"I'm pregnant," Jamie announced.

Bill grinned, then frowned anew. "But you offered me a Seahawks play-off ticket to take her to dinner no more than two or three months ago."

"You paid him to take me to dinner?" Jamie muttered under her breath.

"What can I say?" Rich teased. "I was young and foolish."

"This is all rather sudden, isn't it?" Bill continued, choosing to ignore the whispered conversation between Jamie and Rich.

"Not really," Rich answered. "We've had a fourteen-year courtship."

"Fourteen years!" Bill looked astonished. "It seems congratulations are in order. I couldn't be more pleased for you both."

"Thank you," Jamie returned graciously.

Bill left the office, and Jamie whirled around to face Rich. "You told him we're married!" she cried, her eyes wide and doubting.

"You mean we're not?"

"Rich, we can't be telling your coworkers and not our families."

Rich hadn't given the matter much thought. It hadn't been intentional. But if a husband had just learned he was about to become a father, he should be able to tell someone, and it just so happened that Bill was that someone.

"Since you told Bill," Jamie said, sauntering around his office, "then I should be able to let someone know, too, agreed?" She said it quickly, running the words together.

"Agreed." Personally Rich could see no harm in letting the news out. Especially when the truth was exactly what he was aiming for.

Jamie reached for his phone, hesitated momentarily, then drew in a deep sigh and punched out a phone number. Rich hadn't a clue who she was calling. Personally it didn't matter.

While she was waiting for whomever she'd phoned to answer, Rich moved behind her and wrapped his arms around her waist. It felt good to have her in his arms, and he closed his eyes and drank in the wealth of emotion he experienced when holding her tight. Rubbing his chin across the top of her head, Rich sighed and wondered how long this euphoric feeling would last. All day? A week? As long as a month. Deep down, he began to seriously doubt that it would ever entirely leave him.

So this was love. This warm, full feeling that attacked the senses and the heart. This burning knowledge that the woman you love more than life is nurturing a part of yourself within her womb.

Rich sighed and rubbed his cheek against the side of her neck. She smelled of wildflowers and spring. Lilacs and geraniums. Lilies and orchids.

"Mom, it's Jamie."

Rich tensed. She asked to tell one person and she had opted to tell *her mother*. Rich didn't know Doris Warren well, but what he did remember of her wasn't reassuring. She loved to gossip. Only, she didn't call it that, as he recalled. Women were apt to put a fancy word to it. Doris *networked*.

"Jamie," Rich whispered in her ear. "You're sure you want to do this?"

"Mom, I'm calling because I've got some fabulous news."

"Jamie?" Rich's heart was in a panic.

"I'm pregnant."

He couldn't exactly hear Doris's response, but he knew from the loud, squeaking sound that came from the telephone receiver that Jamie's mother was more than a tad surprised.

"The father?" Jamie repeated the question. She twisted around and grinned sheepishly up at Rich. "That isn't important. What is important is that after all these years, you're finally going to be a grandmother."

"Go ahead and tell her," Rich whispered. Good news, especially news this wonderful, was meant to be shared. Now that Jamie was pregnant, Rich certainly didn't intend on maintaining the confidentiality of their marriage. He couldn't see the point of it. He was too damn proud to keep Jamie's pregnancy under wraps.

"Yes, Mother," Jamie returned, nodding absently. "Of course, I will. No . . . no, not yet."

Listening in on only one half of the conversation put him at a distinct disadvantage, but Rich didn't mind. He was far more interested in spreading nibbling kisses along the side of Jamie's neck.

"Of course I'm sure. One of those home pregnancy tests. . . . Yes, Mother. Listen I have to go now, I'm already late for work. Yes, I'll phone later. Yes, I promise."

Rich's teeth caught hold of Jamie's earlobe and he sucked gently. Her response was immediate; she went weak in his arms. Rich never felt more powerful in his life.

"Rich," she chastised softly.

"Why didn't you tell her we are married?"

"I couldn't...Rich." She playfully swatted her hand at him. She tasted so damn good, he couldn't make himself stop nibbling her neck.

"Why couldn't you tell her?"

"I...I thought I'd break it to her gently, a little at a time."

"So you started off with telling her you're pregnant?" He found her reasoning a bit irrational.

"If I told my mother we were married, she would say something to your parents. We both know she would. Mom's like that."

"I know." The prospect wasn't nearly as intimidating as it had been when Jason had broached the subject with him earlier.

"It'll cause problems."

"No, it won't," Rich countered. He reached for her hand and raised it to his lips, kissing her knuckles. "Because I won't let it."

Jamie glanced regretfully at her watch. "Let's discuss it later. I'm already late for work." She seemed as reluctant to leave as Rich was to let her go.

"Meet me for dinner tonight?" Rich intended to make reservations at the best restaurant in town.

"What time?" Jamie asked.

He tried to judge when he'd be finished, but he had no way of telling. "I won't know until later."

"Don't worry about it. Stop off at my place when you're through here and we can decide then."

Jamie left a few minutes later.

Rich didn't know how her day went, but his was an entire waste. Several times he found himself staring into space, dreaming of Jamie and his child, plotting how long it would take to convince her to let him move in with her and make their marriage real.

His day wouldn't have been so chaotic, though, if he hadn't been slated for meetings for a majority of the afternoon. He'd be taking notes, and before he realized how it happened, his mind would wander to Jamie. He wanted to spend the rest of his life with her, not a few stolen moments out of a hectic work schedule. At the end of the day, he longed to hurry home and find her waiting for him. It didn't take much to envision walking in the front door after a long day at the office and having Jamie there to greet him. Jamie and their son.

That mushy, warm feeling returned, and Rich realized he'd been lost in another world for several minutes. Luckily, he hadn't embarrassed himself at the meetings.

As soon as he'd finished at the office, he hurried out the door. Bill and a couple of the other engineers invited him out for a drink, but Rich declined. He knew his friends were eager to hear the details of his marriage, but he was in too much of a rush to get home.

Home to Jamie. His home and his life. Now all he had to do was convince her how much he loved her and how important she was to him.

Jamie opened the door to him and smiled.

"Hi."

If he didn't know better she seemed almost shy. "Hi, yourself. How are you feeling?"

"The truth?"

Rich nodded. Of course he wanted the truth. He remembered how she'd told him about the dizzy spells and nausea attacks. He'd listened, but in his excitement had forgotten. It didn't occur to him that the pregnancy might have been causing her some physical problems.

"Don't look so worried," she said, laughing gently. "I feel fabulous. Wonderful. I've been walking on air all day."

"Me, too."

"I should never have told my mother, though," she muttered.

If he didn't kiss her soon, Rich realized, he was going to go insane. "Why's that?"

Even as he was asking the question, he was positioning her in his arms. His mouth met hers, and they strained against one another. Eager. Hungry. The kiss moist and hot. His tongue curled around hers. Before he could question the wisdom of his actions, he was unfastening the opening to her blouse. He'd freed four tiny buttons before he had the presence of mind to hesitate.

"Rich?"

"Do you want me to stop?"

"I . . . don't know."

His hand cupped her breast, which was sheathed in a pale cream teddy.

"I thought you'd be starved by this time," she murmured hoarsely.

"I am," he agreed, kissing her once more. Slowly. Thoroughly. Until there could be little doubt of what he wanted. "But it's you I'm hungry for."

"What . . . about dinner?"

"Later," he whispered, easing the silk blouse from her shoulders and reaching for the zipper in the back of her skirt. He rubbed his flattened hands over the plump curve of her buttocks. "I need you, Jamie."

"I need you, too. Oh, Rich, I need you so much."
Her voice was a fleeting whisper.

Rich tracked a row of tiny kisses down the column of
her neck. "Is this what you want?"

"Yes..."

He dipped his tongue into the hollow of her throat.
"How about this?"

"Yes..."

His eased the straps from her teddy over her shoulder, blazing a trail of warm, moist kisses toward her
breast.

The sound of the doorbell went through him like an
electric shock. Jamie tensed. Rich did, too.

"I... I'm not expecting anyone," she said, reaching
for her blouse.

"Don't answer it," Rich advised.

Whoever was on the other side of the door must have
heard him because the buzzer sounded again in a long,
temper-filled blast.

"I'll get rid of whoever it is," she muttered, buttoning her blouse as fast as her fingers would cooperate.
She moved to the front door, checked the peephole,
groaned and rolled away from the door.

"Who is it?" Rich demanded.

Jamie closed her eyes tightly, as though to block out
the sight. "My mother."

Chapter Eleven

"What are we going to do?" Jamie cried, looking to Rich. She'd been such an idiot to announce her pregnancy to her mother. It had been an insane thing to do, but Jamie had been so excited and happy. Keeping such wonderful news to herself for even a minute longer than necessary was too much to bear. Rich had apparently felt the same way because he'd announced their news willy-nilly to a coworker.

They'd both agreed weeks before not to tell anyone about their marriage or the pregnancy until Jamie was five or six months along and her condition was obvious. All that had flown out the proverbial window when Bill Hastings had stepped into Rich's office.

If Rich had found it necessary to announce their marriage, then surely she should be entitled to tell someone about the pregnancy. So Jamie had done what came most naturally; she'd contacted her mother.

"I don't think we have much of an option," Rich stated calmly. "Open the door."

"But . . ." Once again the doorbell buzzed, this time in short repeated taps. There wasn't time to argue, but the prospect of having to face her mother now filled Jamie with dread.

She unbolted the lock and opened the door. "Mother," Jamie greeted, her voice sounding unnaturally high. "This is a pleasant surprise."

Doris Warren's face revealed undisguised dismay. Slowly her gaze traveled to Rich, her eyes rounding even more.

"Hello, Mrs. Warren," Rich said.

"Rich." She nodded stiffly, politely in his direction, then turned toward Jamie, her mouth tightening into a thin line. "You didn't return a single one of my calls, Jamie Marie."

Her mother had called the bank a total of seven times. By the luck of the draw Jamie had managed to avoid having to speak to her. However, she was pragmatic enough to realize she'd need to soon. But first Jamie needed to talk to Rich so they could decide on how much they should explain. That hadn't been possible with Rich tied up in meetings all afternoon.

She'd arrived home, eager to see her husband. Her phone had rung three separate times and she'd let the answering machine take the calls. All three were from her determined mother. Jamie hated having to avoid talking to her own parent, but it was necessary just until she had the chance to talk to Rich. Now the matter had been taken out of her hands.

"Perhaps we should all sit down," Rich suggested, gesturing toward the couch.

"I . . . don't know that I can," Doris Warren muttered. She immediately collapsed onto the thick sofa cushions. "I can't remember when I've ever spent a more distressing day. How could you do such a thing to me?" she accused, glaring at Jamie. "I've been beside myself with questions. My only daughter is having a baby. You're completely sure of this?"

"Yes, Mom, I'm pregnant."

"Who's the father?" Although Doris asked the question, it was more than obvious she suspected Rich. Once again her narrowed gaze traveled to Jamie's husband as though she fully suspected that he would deny the deed.

"I am," Rich announced proudly. He smiled over at Jamie and reached for her hand, squeezing it reassuringly.

Jamie was in the recliner, and Rich sat on the arm, his hand continuing to hold hers.

"There's no need for concern, Mrs. Warren."

"No need for concern!" Jamie's mother shot back heatedly. "I can tell you right now, I most certainly am concerned. This is my daughter you've been fooling around with, and I insist—no, I demand you do the honorable thing."

"Mother!" Jamie had rarely seen her mother more agitated. "Rich isn't a criminal. In case you've forgotten, it takes two to make a baby."

"I did seduce you," Rich delighted in reminding her.

Jamie frowned back at him. "You most certainly did not."

"See," Doris cried, "he admits it."

"What would you like me to do now, Mrs. Warren?" Rich asked, seeming genuinely contrite.

If Jamie didn't know better she'd think he was enjoying this.

"I insist you marry Jamie, of course."

"But are you sure you want me for a son-in-law?"

"I— Yes!"

"Rich!" Jamie was growing downright angry with this silly game of his.

His fingers tightened around hers. Although he did a valiant job of trying to disguise a smile, he failed miserably. His lips quivered and his eyes fairly sparkled. "I believe we'd best tell her, darling."

Darling! Jamie couldn't once remember Rich using the affectionate term. She looked up at him, amazed at his nerve. She was no more his *darling* than the man on the moon.

"Tell me what?" Doris demanded.

"It's complicated." Jamie decided to lead into her marriage to Rich slowly, giving her mother time to adjust to one shock before hitting her with another.

"Life is always complicated," Doris countered, and pinched the bridge of her nose.

"Rich and I have been friends for years."

"The very best of friends," Rich added.

"That much is evident." Jamie's mother raised her chin a notch, as though it demanded a great deal of restraint to remain civil.

"Not evident yet," Rich announced, "but it soon will be."

"What are you doing?" Jamie muttered under her breath.

"Explaining," Rich answered with perfect logic. Then turning to his mother-in-law, he smiled serenely down at Jamie and announced, "There's no need to fear, Mrs. Warren. Jamie and I are already married."

"What?" Doris sprang to her feet. "Jamie, is this true?"

"Yes," she admitted reluctantly. "But I'd hoped to break the news to you a little more gently without shocking you half to death." She glared at Rich, not bothering to cloak her irritation with him.

Her mother sat back down and pressed her hand over her heart as though she couldn't take it all in. "The two of you are married.... When?"

"Several weeks now," Rich answered calmly.

"You didn't say anything—not even to your own mother." This was directed to Jamie.

"There's a perfectly logical explanation why I didn't."

"I can already guess." Doris's hand flew out, her index finger pointed accusingly at Rich. "The two of you *had* to get married."

"That's ridiculous! No one *has* to marry in this day and age." Jamie felt as if she were in a tug-of-war, caught between her mother's shock and her husband's amusement. She wondered if he'd behave the same when it came to informing his own family.

"You are right about one thing," Rich remarked. "Jamie and I did marry for the sake of the child."

"Will you stop!" Jamie vaulted to her feet and brushed her hair away from her face, using both hands.

"Darling..." Rich stared up at her blankly, as though he hadn't a clue to what had caused her outburst.

"Don't darling me!" She turned on him, her aggravation getting the best of her. How Rich could find humor in this situation was beyond her. He made her pregnancy sound like one big joke.

"Jamie, tell me what's going on here." Now it was Doris Warren's turn.

"Rich and I are married," Jamie explained, turning to face her mother. "I would never have agreed to the wedding if Rich hadn't insisted upon it."

"I should certainly hope he insisted."

"You don't understand, and frankly, Mother, I doubt that I can explain now. Let me suffice to say, I'm married and pregnant and you needn't worry about me. I couldn't be happier." Explaining everything at once to her poor confused mother was sure to complicate matters even more than they were already. Someday soon Jamie would answer all her questions, but not now. Not when Rich was acting as though everything were one enormous excuse for amusement.

"You're happy?" Doris's bewildered gaze locked with Jamie's.

"Blissfully." It was Rich who answered for them. It demanded all the fortitude Jamie could muster not to contradict him.

"Then ... I'm happy, too." Doris stood, but seemed surprised to find herself on her feet. She paused and glanced around the room as if she wasn't sure where she was. Taking the cue, Rich walked toward the front door and held it open for her.

"Shall I call you 'Mother'?"

"Ah ..." Doris Warren looked up at him for several awkward moments. "If you wish."

"Goodbye then, Mother Warren. Jamie and I will be in contact with you soon."

As though in a stupor, Jamie's mother walked out the front door. Rich closed it after her. The lock had barely slipped into place when Jamie turned on him.

"What the hell were you doing?" she demanded.

"Reassuring your mother." Rich walked past her and nonchalantly sat in the recliner as though he hadn't a concern in the world. His actions served only to fuel her anger.

"You confused the hell out of her." And Jamie, as well. Just when she was beginning to believe there was a chance of something wonderful developing between them, he'd lapsed into these childish antics of his. The man obviously didn't recognize a crisis when he saw one. "What's wrong with you?" she cried, continuing to pace.

"Wrong?' His eyes went wide with a look of pure innocence.

"You made everything sound like a joke."

"The pregnancy isn't a tragedy. I couldn't be happier. Besides, the sooner we explained everything to your mother, the sooner she'd leave and the sooner we could get back to what we were starting and—"

"You were like this in high school, too." Jamie's anger wasn't going to be appeased that easily. Nor would she allow him to lead her into the bedroom and silence her concerns with a series of slow kisses. There was too much at stake.

"You're going to drag high school into this?"

"Life isn't one big tease, you know."

"I never said it was."

"No," she argued, "you just act that way. We're dealing with my mother and she has—"

"It wasn't me who told her you were pregnant."

"Oh, no," she cried, tossing her hands into the air. "You had to tell Bill Hastings instead."

"That was better than blurting it out to relatives."

"Mom would know soon enough anyway." Jamie noticed the laughter was gone from Rich's eyes and he was beginning to frown.

"If you were looking for me to humbly apologize for my part in this marriage then you've got a long wait. Apparently you have plenty of regrets, but—"

"I didn't say any such thing," Jamie argued.

Rich glared at her. "As I recall, you made a point of announcing how I was the one who'd insisted we marry."

"You *did!*"

Rich ignored her outburst and continued without pause. "You were also the one who insinuated you never wanted the marriage."

"I didn't." Jamie's original idea hadn't included any of this.

From the first, her instincts had told her that marriage, even one of convenience, wasn't to be taken lightly. Rich had never shared her concerns and had carelessly brushed them aside.

"The only reason I went along with this scheme of yours," she reminded him, "was because you insisted."

Fiery anger flashed from his deep blue eyes. "If you're so overwhelmed with regrets, you might have said something sooner."

"I did," she cried. She didn't want to rehash old arguments, but it was apparent they were going to need to clear up the past before they could deal with the future. "I tried to explain my feelings before we were married, but you refused to listen to me. You never do."

"I *never* listen to you?" he challenged.

"Okay, to be fair, you listen, then you brush my worries aside and tell me how foolish I am for being concerned. The wedding is a prime example of that."

"Then why the hell did you agree to it?"

"Because . . . I wanted the baby."

"Then you should be pleased," Rich said as he marched toward the front door. "You've got your baby—it's just me you don't want." With that parting shot, he was gone.

He shut the door with enough force to cause the pictures on the wall to vibrate. Jamie's first instinct was to run after him and tell him she didn't mean any of it. True, she hadn't been keen on the two of them marrying, but for none of the reasons he understood. She loved him, deeply loved him, but she dared not let him know. She needed to remind herself repeatedly that their marriage wasn't a love match. Rich had never intended it to be. She was the one who had problems remembering this was a marriage of convenience.

She was the one who couldn't keep her heart out of their marriage.

Rich had never intended to argue with Jamie. Fighting had been the last thing on his mind when he'd stopped off at her apartment. From the minute she'd left his office that morning, all he could think about was making love to her again. He longed to hold her in his arms and tell her how pleased he was she was pregnant. Nothing had worked out the way he'd plotted. Or wanted. Instead they'd gotten into a shouting match in which she'd repeatedly reminded him how she'd never wanted to marry him in the first place.

She didn't seem particularly concerned about what she was doing to his ego, either.

All right, so maybe his attitude toward Jamie's mother wasn't the best, but he'd be damned if he was going to sit there wearing a dark, brooding frown and pretend this pregnancy was some unthinkable disaster.

So he'd opted for a lighter approach. If Jamie wanted to fault him for that, then fine, he was guilty as charged.

He was a tease. He'd always been a tease. A fact that Jamie had taken delight in reminding him. Leave it to a woman to reach back thirteen years to their high school days and dig up something they could fight about.

Rich walked across his living room, loosening his tie as he moved. His shoulders sagged with an expressive sigh. So, Jamie continued to regret their marriage. No wonder she'd been so eager to offer him the option of a divorce.

He lowered himself into his favorite chair, raised his feet onto the ottoman, leaned his head against the back cushion and closed his eyes. He needed to clear his thoughts, erase any trace of pride and negative emotions. Deal with the issues facing him.

What were the issues?

Jamie was pregnant. Apparently she was as delighted at the prospect as he was himself, but for different reasons. He was a means to the end, and now that he'd accomplished what she wanted, he was of no use to her.

A painful tightening in his chest threatened to suffocate him. He'd met a lot of women in his life. Women who used him, wanted him, manipulated him. He would never have believed Jamie was one of them. It was more than apparent she was looking to push him out of her life. There wasn't much Rich could do.

He couldn't force her to love him.

Rich must have fallen asleep because the next thing he knew the phone was ringing. His eyes shot open, and he stood abruptly, awkwardly and walked across the room. He prayed with everything in him it would be

Jamie phoning, but as he reached for the receiver, he knew it wasn't his headstrong wife.

"Rich?"

It was a questioning, bewildered tone he'd heard in his mother's voice only rarely. "Hello, Mom."

"I just had the most amazing phone call from Doris Warren."

Rich groaned inwardly. "Oh?"

"She's Jamie Warren's mother."

"I know who she is."

"She told me this incredible story about you and Jamie being married?" She made the statement into the form of a question, as if she expected Rich to immediately deny everything.

"She told you that?" Circumstances being what they were, Rich opted to answer his mother's question with one of his own. It seemed the best defense.

"She also said Jamie is pregnant?"

"She said that, too?"

"Is it true?" Like Jamie, his mother had plenty of experience dealing with his stall tactics. When he didn't immediately respond, she raised her voice and asked him again. "Is it?"

Rich wearily brushed a hand down his face, hoping it would help clear his head. "Part of it."

"Which part?" His mother's voice was elevated, quickly advancing toward hysteria. Rich knew his father wasn't there, otherwise Eric Manning would be the one making the call. His mother had a tendency to get excited over the smallest details. For that matter, so did his father.

When his parents had learned Taylor had married Russ Palmer in Reno, all hell had broken loose. They hadn't been thrilled to learn Christy had married Cody

Franklin on the sly, either. Rich could only guess what their reaction would be once they learned he was married to Jamie. Like his two sisters, he'd opted to marry without the traditional family wedding.

"Rather than explain everything over the phone, I suggest Jamie and I stop in first thing tomorrow evening," Rich offered. "We can discuss everything then."

"Tomorrow?"

"I should be able to get away from the office around six. I'll check with Jamie to be sure that that time is convenient for her, as well."

"Just answer one question. Are you and Jamie Warren married or not?"

Rich hesitated, not knowing the truth himself. Not anymore. "Yes and no."

"That doesn't tell me a damn thing," Elizabeth cried.

"I know." Rich couldn't argue with his mother. But he couldn't tell her what he didn't know himself.

When he'd finished the telephone conversation, Rich stared down at the phone for several moments. He didn't have any choice, he had to contact Jamie. Swallowing his pride left a bitter aftertaste in his mouth, but there was no help for it. He reached for the receiver and punched out her number.

Jamie answered on the second ring. Rich didn't bother with any greetings. "I just got a call from my mother. She apparently just finished talking to yours."

Jamie released a slow, frustrated sigh. "I was afraid that would happen. What did you tell her?"

"As little as I could. Naturally she didn't understand. I told her we'd stop in after work tomorrow, around six and explain." Rich attempted to keep the inflection in his voice at a minimum, not allowing any of his emotions to bleed into his words.

"Tomorrow," Jamie repeated.

"If it's inconvenient then I'll let *you* call and explain."

"No... I'll be there."

"I'll see you then." He knew he sounded stiff and formal, but Rich couldn't help it. A man's pride could take only so much of a beating. Jamie had seen to it that he'd received a week's quota all in one conversation.

The line was disconnected and Rich sauntered into his kitchen. He hadn't eaten since early afternoon, and he wasn't particularly hungry. Scanning the contents of his refrigerator, he reached for a cold pop.

On his way out of the kitchen, he paused in front of the phone. Before he could question his actions, he dialed Jason's number and waited the two long rings before his older brother responded.

"Tomorrow night at six," Rich announced without preamble. He wasn't in the mood to exchange polite pleasantries.

"What's happening tomorrow?" Jason demanded, clearly confused.

"I'm telling Mom and Dad I'm married."

Jason's hesitation was only slight. "What brought this on?"

"Jamie's pregnant."

"But I thought she canceled the appointment with—"

"She did." Rich realized he sounded abrupt and disagreeable. Hell, he *was* abrupt and disagreeable. Jason had asked to be included when Rich told their parents about his and Jamie's wedding.

"But if Jamie canceled the doctor's appointment, then how..."

"This baby was conceived in the traditional way."

Jason was silent for a moment. "You don't sound happy about it."

"I couldn't be more pleased," Rich snapped. "I'm happy. Real happy."

But it didn't seem a fair exchange. He wanted the baby; he couldn't be more pleased Jamie was pregnant, but nothing was happening the way he would have liked. If the evening had gone the way Rich had hoped, he and Jamie would be in bed together right this minute. They'd be wrapped in each other's arms. Her face would be nestled on his shoulder, and when they kissed, it would be a leisurely exploration of their need and appreciation of one another. His restless hands would roam at will over her lush womanly body, and he'd spread his palm over her flat satin-smooth stomach, communicating his love to his unborn son. When they made love, it would be a celebration of their joy over her pregnancy.

Only Jamie didn't need him any longer.

Rich had served his purpose.

Rich had trouble keeping his mind on his work the following afternoon. Every ten minutes or so, he found his gaze wandering to his watch. Each time, he mentally calculated how long it would be before he'd be forced to confront his parents with the truth.

A little after five, he was sitting at his desk, reviewing some figures when there was a polite knock at his door. He grumbled a reply, and the door slowly creaked open.

Jamie stood before him, dressed in a pretty pink suit. "Is this a bad time?"

The last person Rich expected to come waltzing through his office door was his pregnant wife. Seeing her now took him by surprise.

"No," he said, rolling back his chair, "you're not disturbing a thing." Maybe his equilibrium . . . and his heart. But precious little else. "Sit down." He gestured toward the chair on the other side of his desk.

Jamie sat down, and he noted her gaze fell to her clenched hands.

"What brings you here?"

"I—I thought we should discuss what we are going to tell your parents."

It was a logical enough excuse to seek him out, Rich supposed. Not very original, but real enough. "What do you suggest?" He hoped to give the impression that whatever they decided didn't matter one way or the other to him. He leaned against the back of the chair and locked his fingers at his nape.

"Do they know I'm pregnant?"

"Your mother took delight in telling mine you were."

"I thought she must have," Jamie said, releasing an elongated sigh. "I feel like such a fool."

"Why?"

She shrugged, still avoiding eye contact. "For blurting it out that way. I've muddled everything."

Rich didn't agree or disagree. It seemed every time he opened his mouth he said something he shouldn't. Heaven forbid if he were to make a joke of it.

"How much do you plan to explain?" Jamie asked, risking a glance in his direction.

Rich hadn't decided that. "Everything," he said off the top of his head.

"A-all of it?"

"All. I can't see any reason to hold any of it back." A little of the disappointment and lingering animosity from their argument from the day before seeped into his words.

"I thought that we might want them to assume that the baby—"

"No," Rich answered forcefully.

Jamie's startled gaze connected with his. "You didn't even let me finish."

"I already knew what you were going to say. You want my parents to assume this baby was conceived artificially. I won't be a party to that."

"That isn't what I intended."

Rich's phone rang just then. Rich automatically reached for it, although he would have preferred to ignore it.

"Engineering," he responded automatically.

"It's Paul," his eldest brother announced. "I just got done talking to Mom. What the hell's going on between you and Jamie Warren?"

"Nothing." So Mom was calling in the big guns. Paul was the responsible one in the family, not that Jason and Rich weren't. But when it came to family problems, his parents tended to lean on Paul for support.

"That's not what I heard," Paul insisted. "I got a call from Mom no more than ten minutes ago with some crazy rumor about you being married."

"It's no rumor."

"Jamie Warren?"

"Jamie Warren Manning," Rich answered without thinking. He had to stop thinking of Jamie in those terms. She would never be a Manning. Rich could feel her stare, but he avoided glancing in her direction, refusing to give her the power to disconcert him.

"Mom claims Jamie's pregnant."

"She is." Rich had no intention of hiding the fact. Within a few months, Jamie's condition would become obvious. Jamie might prefer to hide behind a brick wall, sugarcoating the truth, but he wanted no part of it.

"Why the hell didn't you tell anyone?" Paul wanted to know.

"That's a long story."

"I hope you intend on telling it tonight." Paul sounded a good deal like their father, Rich noted. It wasn't a role the eldest Manning assumed often. He was baffled by Rich's actions and didn't bother to disguise his disappointment.

Rich rubbed his hand across his eyes. No thanks to Jamie, he hadn't slept well the night before. His dreams had been troubling, and he'd tossed restlessly until morning.

"Jamie and I'll be there at six. We'll explain everything then."

"Good. I plan on being there, as well."

Briefly Rich closed his eyes to the mounting frustration. This meeting with his parents was becoming a real zoo with Paul and Jason sitting on the sidelines. Rich wouldn't be surprised if his parents brought in Taylor and Christy, too.

His whole family was about to discover that Rich was the biggest fool who'd ever walked the face of the earth.

Chapter Twelve

Both of Rich's brothers were there waiting for him when he arrived at his parents' home with Jamie at five minutes of six. Paul and Jason were perched on bar stools, holding pop cans, enthusiastically eager to view the latest family side show. The scene reminded Rich of one that had been played out months earlier between his parents and his sister Christy when she'd announced her marriage to Cody Franklin. Rich remembered being highly amused by the circumstances then. Following in his youngest sister's footsteps, however, was proving to be far less comfortable.

His mother was busy on the phone, and from the way she was shaking her head and muttering under her breath, Rich realized she was probably talking to one of his sisters in Montana.

Rich walked into the living room with Jamie at his side. He noted how close she stood to him, which surprised him. While still at his office, they'd taken several minutes to review exactly what they planned to say.

To him, the entire matter was cut-and-dried. He was in his thirties, certainly old enough to do as he damn well pleased without his parents' approval. Who and why Rich had married was his own business, and that was how he intended to keep it. He'd convinced Jamie he intended to blurt out the details of their arrangement to his family, but he sincerely doubted it would come to that.

After Rich and Jamie were seated, Eric Manning walked out of the kitchen and into the living room. His father was tall and in excellent physical condition, Rich noted with pride. His thick hair was nearly all gray, and his hairline had barely begun to recede. He seemed to be in robust health.

Rich's two sisters claimed all the men in the Manning family were black-belt chauvinists. Rich hadn't given much thought to the matter, but he had definite ideas when it came to the weaker sex.

Weaker sex.

That was enough to make him laugh. Jamie could wrap him around her little finger with a word. Hell, she could do it with a look. If anyone could be accused of being weak, it wasn't the Jamies of this world.

"Rich," his father said, nodding once. Eric's face was tight, and the glance he shot toward Rich would have quelled Attila the Hun.

"Dad." Rich chose to sit on the sofa. Jamie was at his side. He didn't know whose hand reached out first, but their fingers entwined naturally, as though they needed each other. As though they would gain strength from one another. Jamie appeared far more nervous than Rich, which, he supposed, was natural.

"Your mother's talking to Taylor," his father explained. "She'll be finished in a few minutes."

So Rich had guessed correctly. His mother had managed to involve his oldest sister in this.

"Would you care for something to drink?" Eric asked Jamie. "There's some cold pop, coffee or tea."

"Nothing, thanks," she answered with a gentle smile.

Rich noticed that Jamie briefly rested her free hand against her stomach, then drew in a deep, calming breath.

"Are you feeling all right?" She'd once mentioned not being well in the mornings, but he'd been so caught up in his own concerns that the matter had slipped his mind.

"I'm fine."

"You're looking pale." This was something else he noted.

"It's nerves."

"What about mornings?"

Rich wasn't especially thrilled to have his two brothers and his father monitoring his conversation, but he was concerned about Jamie and ultimately their baby's health.

"My stomach's a little queasy yet, but I heard it'll get better in a few months."

"The book I've been reading claims morning sickness should gradually disappear starting at about the third month." Rich had devoured the paperback on pregnancy and childbirth all in one sitting, eager to read everything he could about the changes taking place inside Jamie's womb. Eager to discover the most minute details of how his child was forming.

Jamie's eyes brightened. "You're reading a book?"

"It might surprise you to learn I read quite a bit," he chided.

"I know," she whispered, and her gaze met his, faltering slightly. "I guess I'm surprised you're reading one about pregnancy and birth."

"Why should that amaze you?"

She shrugged. "It just does."

That didn't say much of her view of him. Rich would have questioned her further, but his mother chose to saunter into the room just then. Elizabeth Manning smiled warmly in Jamie's direction, but her eyes hardened as they slid toward Rich. He didn't know what he'd done that was so terrible. His father had viewed him in much the same way, as though he should be taken around to the woodpile and have his backside tanned. The thought was almost comical.

"How's Taylor?" Rich inquired conversationally, ignoring the censured looks coming from both his parents. He kept his voice cool and even. He was actually proud of the composure that reverberated in his own words.

"Taylor's fine. So are Russ and little Eric."

"That's great." Rich crossed his long legs and leaned against the back of the couch. This wasn't going to be nearly as bad as he suspected as long as he managed to keep a cool head.

"Taylor's decided to do some substitute teaching for the school district. Unfortunately Russ isn't keen on the idea, but he's coming around."

Rich knew from experience that his oldest sister's will was powerful enough to launch spacecrafts. Russ would do well to recognize as much and react accordingly.

"She was surprised to hear you and Jamie are married," his mother continued, after drawing in a deep breath. "Which, I might add, came as a significant shock to your father and me, as well."

"Not me." Jason spoke for the first time. "I knew about it from the beginning. In fact, I was Rich's best man."

Everyone's attention swung accusingly to Jason.

"You knew?" their mother echoed.

Jason nodded profoundly. "Trust me. I tried to talk him out of this craziness, but you know how stubborn Rich can be. He refused to listen to the advice of his betters."

"You asked Jason to the ceremony and not your own mother?" Elizabeth Manning cried. She reached for a tissue and dabbed it at the corner of her eyes, as though to suggest she'd failed miserably as a mother.

"It was a civil ceremony at the King County Courthouse," Rich started to explain. He didn't get very far. Once again he was interrupted by his mother.

"You didn't even marry Jamie in a church?" Elizabeth made it sound as if this were the worst deed of all.

"Don't be upset, Mrs. Manning, I preferred it be that way," Jamie answered, her voice incredibly soft.

"But...why get married in a courthouse when you've both been raised in the Church?"

Jamie turned nervously to Rich. Now was the time to announce the reason for their impromptu wedding.

Rich had it all worked out in his mind. The assurances, the brief but concise explanation of what had led up to their unusual agreement. Yet when the moment arrived, Rich discovered he couldn't make himself say it.

"We did it that way for our own reasons," was all the explanation he was willing to give. From the corner of his eye, Rich caught sight of Jason arching his brows as if to say he was surprised Rich opted to mask the details.

"According to Jamie's mother, Jamie was already pregnant at the time of the wedding," Eric bellowed. With his hands clenched at his sides, he paced the length of the living room, then paused in front of the floor-to-ceiling windows, his back to Jamie and Rich. "A couple doesn't need any more excuse to marry quickly than that."

"I hate to disillusion you both," Rich reported calmly, "but as a matter of fact, Jamie wasn't pregnant when we married."

Elizabeth glared at him, her look suggesting it was all a lie. Rich had no intention of arguing with either of his parents; they could believe what they wished.

"Then why did Doris make a point of telling us the two of you had married because of the baby?"

Rich groaned inwardly. His cockiness had gotten him into more pots of hot water than he cared to count. "Because basically we'd decided Jamie should become pregnant as soon as possible."

Jamie shared a brief look with Rich, and added, "We married because we both long to become parents."

"I tried to tell them a wedding wasn't necessary," Jason inserted, "but they wouldn't listen to me. Apparently they felt if they were going to have a baby they should marry first. Go figure."

His mother gave Jason a horrified look. "I should certainly hope so."

Eric turned around to face them and frowned. "Trust me, parenthood's not all it's cracked up to be."

"Come on, Dad," Paul teased. "It hasn't been so bad, now has it?"

"When it comes to raising teenagers and weddings," Eric argued, "it's been a nightmare. It was bad enough that your sisters had to marry without the benefit of family, but I never suspected one of you boys would pull that stunt. I want to know when the hell there's going to be a real wedding in this family."

"Diane and I had a real wedding," Paul reminded his father.

"But no one from the Manning family was there." Eric's voice boomed like a cannon shot. "The boy goes into the army, is shipped off to Alaska and returns home a married man."

"It was just one of those things," Paul said, grinning.

"Getting back to Rich and Jamie," their mother said pointedly.

"By all means," Jason agreed, gesturing toward the sofa, his pop can in his hand. "Let's get back to Rich and Jamie. Do Mom and Dad realize they're married and aren't even living together?"

Rich tossed his brother a look hot enough to form glass.

"Rich?" His mother looked to him expectantly.

"Not living together? Why the hell not? You're married aren't you?" His father fired rapid questions at them, one following on the heels of the other.

"We're married," Rich confirmed.

"But you're not living together?"

"Not . . . yet." This was the best evasion tactic Rich could come up with on such short notice. This was a subject he'd hoped to avoid along with a list of several others.

"It's apparent they plan to move in together, isn't that right, Rich?" His mother looked expectantly toward him.

"Of course." It was Jamie who responded, causing Rich to pause and stare at her. He couldn't help wondering if she was sincere or if her sudden reassurances were all part of an act to appease his parents. Not that Rich had any objections about moving in with Jamie. It was something he'd given a good deal of thought to since their marriage.

"Are there problems with your lease?" his mother inquired.

"I'm working on it," Rich muttered noncommittally.

"I should hope you'll move in with her soon," Eric asserted, burying his hands in his pants pockets. "A pregnant woman needs her husband."

"You're absolutely positive you're pregnant, Jamie dear?" Elizabeth Manning asked the question with gentle concern.

"Absolutely positive," Jamie confirmed. "The kit I bought at the drugstore has a narrow probability of error, but I was at the doctor's this afternoon and he confirmed my condition."

"You went to the doctor?" Rich asked before he could stop himself. They'd spent a half hour or more at his office discussing this meeting and she hadn't said a word about having seen Dr. Fullerton.

"It was a short visit."

"Did he give you a due date?"

Jamie smiled shyly and nodded.

"When?" Rich was mentally calculating dates. His best guess placed her delivery date sometime close to

Christmas. A son would make for a priceless gift to place under a gaily decorated tree.

"The last week of December," Jamie announced.

"I always did love the winter months," Rich remarked, having a difficult time keeping the pride and elation from affecting his voice. Then, damning his pride and caution, he brought her knuckles up to his mouth and brushed his lips over the top of Jamie's hand.

Elizabeth sighed softly. "Are you experiencing bouts of morning sickness, my dear?"

"A few."

"A husband should be with his wife," Eric reminded Rich for the second time.

"We've been discussing Rich moving in with me," Jamie announced. This was certainly news to Rich, who couldn't recall a single word of such a conversation. After Doris Warren had unexpectedly stopped by Jamie's apartment, they'd barely been able to talk to one another.

"I've got a truck," Jason reminded them, once again motioning toward them with his aluminum pop can. "Any time you need anything hauled, little brother, just say the word."

"I will," Rich promised. He didn't know what Jamie was up to, but he wasn't complaining. If she wanted his family to assume this was a love match, he'd play along with her. He knew the truth, but this was an unexpected turn for the better.

"It's settled, then," Eric said forcefully. "Rich is moving in with Jamie."

"Shouldn't we hold a reception in their honor?" Rich's mother asked his father. Her eyes were sparkling with excitement. Rich remembered how his mother had thrown all her efforts into the engagement party for Christy and what a disaster that had turned out to be.

"We should leave that up to these young folks, don't you think?"

Rich wasn't keen on a reception, especially in light of the fact Jamie was planning on divorcing him as soon as their baby was born. Thank heaven no one had gotten around to inquiring about their marriage arrangement.

Rich made a point of glancing at his watch. "If you'll both excuse us, Jamie told her mother we'd be stopping by her house, as well." She delivered that tidbit of information when she'd arrived at his office earlier in the afternoon.

The prospect of facing Doris Warren a second time in as many days didn't thrill Rich. One set of parents at a time was about all he could handle.

Jamie didn't know what had caused her to lie to Rich's family. Normally she stuck to the truth, believing with all her being that a lie was always wrong. Yet when Rich's father had started questioning them about their living arrangements, Jamie found herself perpetuating a falsehood.

Rich looked flabbergasted when she announced they planned on moving in together. Stunned. To his credit, he recovered quickly and played along with her as though they'd only recently reached such a decision.

Although they hadn't once discussed the prospect, Jamie had hoped Rich would suggest moving in with her once he learned she was pregnant. He hadn't, though.

Jamie deeply regretted their argument from the day before. A hundred times during the long sleepless night, she'd played back their angry exchange and felt all the more dreadful.

She'd overreacted. Rich was only being Rich. She'd condemned him because he'd chosen to deal with a tense situation with humor.

His parting shot about her not wanting him now that she was pregnant was what had troubled her the most. He couldn't honestly believe that. Jamie was crazy about Rich. She'd been in love with him for years, only she'd been too blind to recognize it.

Following her appointment with Dr. Fullerton, Jamie had stopped off at Rich's office at the Boeing Renton complex. She'd hoped they'd have a few minutes alone so they could clear the air. But when she arrived, Rich was stone cold and just about as friendly.

Only when they were at his parents' home did he lower his guard. He'd taken her hand in his and smiled down on her as though they'd never exchanged a cross word. Of course it could all be for show, but Jamie prayed that wasn't the case.

"Your mother seems to be in better spirits this evening," Rich commented conversationally. He drove at a relaxed pace, weaving through the narrow neighborhood streets.

"She's had time to adjust to our news." Their visit had been short and sweet. Just long enough to offer the reassurances her mother seemed to need. Playing the role of the happy mother-in-waiting wasn't the least bit difficult for Jamie.

"Have you adjusted to the news?" Rich surprised her by asking.

"Yes. What about you?"

Rich nodded. "I suppose I should be surprised, but frankly, I'm not. By the way, are you hungry?"

"A little." Actually Jamie was famished. She'd woken with a queasy stomach that morning and opted to skip breakfast. Then at noon, she'd eaten a small carton of blueberry yogurt, but that had been hours before.

"Do you want to stop off and get something to eat?"

"No," she said, thinking quickly. "We could order pizza and have it delivered to my place."

He glanced her way as if the suggestion had astonished him. "That sounds good to me."

It was nearly eight by the time they arrived at Jamie's condominium. While Rich ordered the pizza, Jamie went into her bedroom and changed out of her crisp business suit. She chose jeans and a pale blue sweater.

By the time she returned to the living room, Rich had loosened his tie and was glancing through the evening paper. He looked up when she entered the room and slowly set the newspaper aside.

"I hope you realize both sets of parents fully expect me to move in with you now." He said it as if the thought was heavy on his mind.

"I know." She sat across from him, leaned forward and clenched her hands. "Personally I...don't think it's such a bad idea."

"You don't?" He didn't sound as if he believed her.

"I mean...this will probably be the only pregnancy for either of us, and since you've been reading so much about it, and seem so interested...it's only fair that you share as much of the experience as possible." Jamie hesitated a moment. "Unless of course, you'd rather not live with me."

He gave a noncommittal shrug. "I don't have any objection." His gaze moved past her to the hallway that led to the two bedrooms. "Naturally I'll be sleeping in the spare bedroom."

"Naturally," Jamie concurred. But not for long, if everything went as she hoped. She loved Rich. Truly loved him. Thus far, she'd bungled their relationship and their marriage at every turn. If he were to share these short precious months with her before the birth of their child, there was a chance he might grow to love her, as well.

It was worth the risk.

Worth the potential for heartache.

Worth chancing her pride and her future for this one opportunity.

The pizza arrived, and they sat at the kitchen table, the square cardboard box propped open in front of them. Both Rich and Jamie chose to drink tall glasses of cold milk.

"So you've been feeling queasy in the mornings?" Rich posed the question after several minutes of comfortable silence. He too seemed to be working as hard as Jamie to maintain this fragile peace.

"Only a little. Dr. Fullerton said it would pass soon enough. I haven't gotten really sick."

"Good."

"Dr. Fullerton suggested I nibble on a couple of soda crackers when I first wake up."

"I can bring them in to you, if you like."

Jamie nodded. She would like that, but she was afraid to let Rich know how much it would mean to her. Even now, weeks later, she continued to miss their early-morning phone conversations. They'd shared a special closeness then, one that was sadly missing of late.

"Would you like a cup of coffee?" Jamie asked when they'd finished.

Rich nodded.

"Go ahead and read the newspaper and I'll bring it in to you."

"That's a nice, wifely thing to do."

"Yes, it is, isn't it?" Jamie answered with a saucy smile. She took her time assembling the pot of coffee. While she waited for the water to seep through the grounds, she cleaned the kitchen, wiped down the counters and placed their few dishes into the dishwasher.

Carrying a steaming cup of coffee into the living room, she hesitated when she found Rich's eyes were closed. The newspaper was clenched in his hands as though he were reading each and every word.

Smiling to herself, Jamie sat on the ottoman and crossed her legs. Taking a sip of the coffee, she carefully studied the man she'd married. His features were more relaxed now. His head cocked slightly to one side.

How handsome he was. His good looks even more appealing in slumber. Not certain what dictated her actions, Jamie set the coffee aside and slipped the newspaper from his unsuspecting grasp. Rich stirred briefly, then nestled more securely in the chair, supporting his head against the back cushion.

Jamie reached for the light, dimming it. Then, calling herself a romantic idiot, she slipped into Rich's lap and pressed her head against his shoulder.

"Jamie?" He sounded unsure.

"Were you looking to find someone else in your arms?" she asked in a small whisper.

"No." A smile faintly curved his mouth.

His grin disappeared as his hand framed her face, and his pale blue eyes held hers captive. Jamie could feel her heart pound frantically against her rib cage. His thumb caressed the line of her jaw.

"I never realized how beautiful you are."

Jamie dropped her gaze, afraid to meet his eyes. She wasn't anywhere close to being beautiful, and it hurt, a good kind of hurt, that he should think otherwise.

His mouth sought out hers. The kiss began slow and gentle, so gentle that Jamie could feel herself begin to melt. A feeling of sublime languor filled her. It was completely unfair, downright decadent that he should make her feel such things over a simple kiss.

Simple. Rich didn't know the meaning of the word. Certainly not when it came to kissing.

His tongue played at the seam of her mouth until she willingly parted her lips for him. He groaned, then slowly guided his tongue into the cavern of her mouth. The warm host of sensations increased in intensity as she curled her tongue around his. Heat intertwined with heat. Moisture with moisture. Excitement with excitement.

Jamie heard the whimpering sound long before she recognized it came from herself.

Rich ended the kiss as leisurely as he had begun it. Jamie's eyes remained closed, and her breathing came in staggered gasps. For long, priceless moments, he held her. His fingers were at the back of her head, stroking her hair. In those few short moments, Jamie felt the air vibrate with sweet, unspoken promises.

He wanted to make love to her.

Jamie wanted it, too.

"I should be heading home?" Rich's voice lifted softly at the end of his statement, turning it into a question.

"No," she whispered, catching his lower lip between her teeth and sucking gently.

"No?"

"You're moving in with me, remember?"

"Starting tonight?"

"Starting right this moment."

"You're sure?"

Jamie smiled and pressed her lips to his, then penetrated his mouth with the provocative tip of her tongue. "You want to argue with me?"

"No...it's just..."

She didn't allow him to finish, kissing him once more, soundly this time, cramming her heart, her soul, her love into a single kiss.

She surprised him. His soft gasp confirmed as much. He groaned anew, then plunged his tongue hungrily forward to duel with her own. His elbows were braced against her sides, digging into her ribs, and his fingers were buried deep in her hair.

They were both trembling when the kiss ended.

Slipping off his lap, Jamie stood and held out her hand to Rich. His smoky, passion-hazed eyes searched out hers, his gaze questioning.

"You're sure?" he asked her once again, his words ragged with need, his eyes hot with passion and some other emotion she couldn't read. Restraint? Doubt? Jamie didn't know which.

"I'm sure."

"You're already pregnant."

Why he felt the need to remind her of that was beyond her understanding. "Yes, I know." As she was speaking, her hands were busy unfastening the buttons of his shirt. Rich helped her by pulling his tie loose and dropping it to the carpet. Jamie slid the shirt from his shoulders, then ran her hands down the full length of his arms.

His chest captured her attention next. His muscular, warm chest. She ran her flattened hands over the smooth, hair-roughened skin, marveling at the strength she sensed in him. She closed her eyes, wanting him so badly she felt weak with the need.

"You make me crazy."

"I do?" It made no sense to Jamie.

"Yes. I want you so much you make me ache."

"I know.... You make me ache, too."

Rich groaned and reached for her, cupping her buttocks with his hands and lifting her against him until she became profoundly aware of the heated length of his arousal.

For one wild second it was as though the world stood still for them. Still and quiet. Rich's blue eyes appeared aquamarine in the dim light. Bright and intense, filled with a wealth of need, a wealth of promises.

Jamie felt completely vulnerable to him. Vulnerable and desirable, more desirable than she'd ever felt in her life. She smiled and stepped away from him.

Rich looked utterly confused, but he released her.

Jamie turned away and had gone two steps before she twisted around. A smile quivered at the edges of her mouth. "You coming?"

"Where are you going?"

She laughed softly, sexily, and held out her hand to him. "You mean you don't know?"

Chapter Thirteen

Rich stirred in the middle of the night. It took him only a matter of seconds to realize he was in bed with Jamie. For the next several minutes he did nothing more than watch his wife as she slept. He soaked in every delicate nuance of her beauty. His thirsty eyes drank freely of her, as though they'd been separated by time and distance, when in actuality she'd spent the majority of the night in his arms.

Gradually his gaze lowered to her lips, parted slightly, her breathing slow and even. She had the most delectable mouth, all sweet and soft and ever so pliable against his own.

Desire came at him unexpectedly, its sharp talons cutting at him. Memories of the warm gentle way Jamie had led him to her bed came to him like the mist surrounding a full moon. She'd held her arms out to him, until the ache of wanting her, needing her, ate away at him, dissolved any will he had to refuse her.

She'd freely opened her heart and her body to him. When she'd cried out in pleasure at her completion, the sound of her joy had pierced his very soul. The sheer, utter beauty of their lovemaking had marked him in ways he was only beginning to understand.

Jamie stirred softly and rolled her head to one side. Her hair spilled across her face, and after a moment, Rich risked waking her by gently brushing it aside. His breathing came fast and hard. Much too fast for such a simple task as touching his wife's face.

Before he could stop himself, he leaned forward, intending to kiss her. The way he was feeling, with need clawing at his insides, he knew if he followed through with his intention, the kiss would be harsh, volatile. By a supreme act of his will, he stopped himself just in time.

Sweet heaven, he'd made love to her only hours before and already he was wondering how long it would be before he could take her again.

He needed to think. Pull himself together. Make some sense of this nagging physical ache, before he woke Jamie and frightened her. Throwing aside the covers, he sat on the side of the mattress, leaned forward and rubbed his hands down his face. He needed something to help him clear his head.

"Rich."

The soft panic he heard in Jamie's voice caused him to turn around.

"Don't leave me," she pleaded, her voice little more than a whisper. "Not again."

"I wasn't going to." He slipped back into the bed and gathered her in his arms. She felt so damn soft against him. Just holding her left him feeling solid and powerful.

"Don't go," she repeated, almost delirious, clinging to him.

"I can't." Even if he'd wanted to, Rich could never walk away from her. He was so much in love with her, it was driving him insane.

He kissed her, hoping to reassure her, but the kiss was everything he'd feared. And wanted. His mouth was hard and demanding, his hands investigating her warm, perfect skin as his mouth ravaged hers.

"Jamie..." He dragged his mouth down the perfume-scented curve of her neck, down her shoulder to the peaked softness of her breast.

Jamie moaned softly and arched her back, encouraging him, offering him more and more. He caught her nipple between his lips and sucked deeply, taking more and more of her into his hot mouth.

Jamie plowed her fingers through his hair and thrashed beneath him.

He lifted his head and kissed her mouth. "I need you... again," he whispered, trapping the words between their straining, eager lips.

Their need for one another was as urgent as their kisses. A strangled cry slipped from her throat as her nails clawed at his back.

Rich jerked his mouth from hers. "I'm frightening you?" He feared he had, or worse, that he was hurting her.

"No... no, love me, just love me."

"I intend to."

Rich intended to do a whole lot more than simply fulfill their bodies' hunger. But for then, his need was too great to take it slow. Or easy. Or any other way.

Ruthless desire dictated his actions. He craved to fill the hollowness that ate at his soul, and to end the interminable loneliness that had marked his life.

She was so damned soft, sprawled as she was, her legs, her heart open and vulnerable to him. Her dark hair was fanned about her shoulders. Her sweet face was flushed with excitement, her eyes wide and misty with an emotion too strong to voice. Her lips were parted and moist from his kisses, and her breath came in tiny gasps of encouragement.

Rich couldn't resist her a second longer. Not another second.

"Oh . . . Jamie." He clenched his teeth as he slipped into the warm cradle of her womanhood. Her moist, inviting cradle. She took in the full, throbbing length of him until he was buried in her. Buried in her gentleness. Buried in the moist warmth of her heart.

Rich had never known a pleasure more intense. He didn't dare move, didn't dare breathe.

Soon he discovered it wasn't necessary for him to move. Jamie did it for him, wiggling her hips, rotating and lifting her buttocks. The sounds coming from her were wild and guttural, half-formed words of encouragement, half-spoken pleas, whispered promises.

"Jamie . . ." He growled her name when he could, readjusting himself above her, realigning their bodies, sheathing himself deeply within her. "Yes . . . yes . . . ah, Jamie, just like that . . . ." He didn't know how she managed it, but with one tiny twist of her hips, she was able to take him in more fully.

"Please . . . oh, please." She thrashed her head against the pillow. "Yes . . . yes."

"Jamie . . . love . . . my love."

* * *

The alarm rang crankily while it was still dark. Jamie rolled onto her side and blindly reached toward the clock radio, shutting off the irritating beep.

Rich rolled toward her, cradling her spoon fashion, looping his arm around her middle. "Good morning," he whispered on the tail end of a yawn. With familiarity, his hand cupped her breast. Although they'd spent the majority of the night making love, Jamie was amazed at her body's ready response to his touch.

"Morning." Jamie couldn't help feeling a little shy after the tempestuous night they'd spent. Memories of their lovemaking filled her mind like water saturating a dry sponge. The brazen way she'd led him into her bedroom, stripped for him, stripped him, caused her cheeks to fill with color.

"How are you feeling this morning?" Rich asked, his mouth close to her ear. He caught her lobe between his teeth and sucked gently, shooting warm shivers down Jamie's spine.

"I'm fine."

"Do you want me to bring you some soda crackers?"

Jamie hadn't realized he was asking her about the baby. "Not...yet." She eased back the covers and cautiously righted herself. When she did suffer bouts of nausea, it was generally when she first sat up. With her legs dangling over the edge of the mattress, she inhaled a deep breath and was pleased to discover she felt fine.

"Do you want to shower first?" Rich asked from behind her, his hands at her waist.

"Please." She had trouble looking at him. It was silly, she realized, to be nervous. They were married, for heaven's sake. Married. There wasn't any reason to feel edgy or ill at ease. Rich was her husband, and he had a perfect right to spend the night with her.

Jamie moved into her bathroom and turned on the shower, adjusting its temperature. It wasn't until she was under the pulsating spray that she remembered.

The scene replayed itself for her, its effect as brutal as a cold slap across the face.

Rich had intended on leaving her again, sneaking out in the middle of the night. If she hadn't stirred when she did, he would have walked out on her a second time. Once again he had planned on leaving her to face the morning alone. Only this time she'd woken and had pleaded with him to stay.

Jamie didn't know how long she stood under the spray. Long enough to adjust her breathing and wait for the pain that rippled through her to subside.

When she finished, she pasted on a smile and walked nonchalantly back into the bedroom, a fresh white towel hugging her torso like a second skin. "Your turn," she announced with forced cheerfulness.

Rich had made the coffee and had brought her in a mug, along with a small plate with four soda crackers. "Breakfast is served," he said, bowing before her.

Jamie reached for the coffee, being careful to keep the towel securely in place with one hand. It was ludicrous to be modest after what they'd shared. The things they'd said. The beautiful things they'd done.

Nevertheless she was.

Rich frowned briefly, then left her. Although the bathroom door was securely shut, Jamie heard him singing at the top of his lungs above the sound of the shower. With only a few undisturbed minutes offered her, she quickly dressed, haphazardly choosing her outfit for the day.

She made up the bed, placed Rich's scattered clothes on top and then hurriedly moved into the kitchen. Generally she didn't pack a lunch, but she did so this morning, just to help pass the time. If there was anything to be grateful for, it was that Rich hadn't called her darling. He'd only done that in the presence of others. He was a lot of things, but a hypocrite wasn't one of them.

She was putting together a sandwich when Rich joined her. He poured himself a second cup of coffee. Jamie concentrated on assembling her turkey sandwich and managed to avoid eye contact with him.

She turned around, intending on taking an apple from the refrigerator and stopped short of colliding with Rich. "Oh, sorry," she mumbled under her breath, flattening herself against the counter so he could move past her.

"Would you like some breakfast?" she asked matter-of-factly, as though she often made the same inquiry of men who spent the night with her.

"Just coffee, thanks."

Jamie sighed with relief. The intimacy of cooking a meal for him would have been a strain. She made a point of glancing at her watch. "I guess I'd better head to the salt mines," she said, striving to sound carefree and happy when all the while there was a lump in her throat the size of a goose egg.

"Me, too." Rich's voice was low and hesitant, as if he wasn't quite sure what was happening, but whatever it was, he didn't like it.

Jamie didn't, either, but she didn't know how to change it.

She was halfway out of the kitchen when Rich stopped her.

"I'll have to leave with you."

"Why?" She was eager to escape, willing to do anything so she could be by herself, examine her thoughts, analyze what was happening between them.

His smile didn't quite reach his eyes. "I don't have a key to lock up with."

"Oh, right." She opened the closet door and reached for her coat, holding on to it as if it were protection.

"If I'm going to move in with you, it might be a good idea to have one made for me."

"Moving in with me." She'd made the suggestion when they'd met with Rich's family. It had seemed like a good idea at the time, and she'd been so eager to find a way to make her marriage work.

"I take it you've changed your mind?"

"No," she countered hastily. "I . . . just think we should reevaluate the situation before we do something we might both regret later."

" 'Regret later,' " Rich repeated slowly, the words packed with restrained violence. "In other words, you regret ever having made the offer."

"I didn't say that."

"You didn't have to." He moved past her and out the front door, slamming it behind him. The sound reverberated off the walls like thunder, leaving Jamie alone to withstand the storm.

Rich had never met a more contrary woman in his life. One minute his sweet wife was holding out her arms to him, leading him into her bedroom. And in the next she was behaving as though she couldn't get away from him fast enough.

Rich wasn't the one who'd announced to his family that they were moving in together. Nor was he the one who invited himself into her home for dinner and then seduced him. All right, she hadn't exactly seduced him, but the lovemaking had been Jamie's idea, as well.

Then, in the bright light of morning, she acted as though she'd never seen him before. As though she would have appreciated it if he'd disappeared in the middle of the night.

Leaving before she woke was what had gotten him in trouble the first time they'd made love.

Rich was damned if he did and damned if he didn't.

He didn't understand it. He'd never known a woman who confused him more.

To his credit, Rich tried to work, but my midmorning he felt like calling it quits for the day. Leaning back in his chair, he rubbed his hand down the length of his face. Generally, when he had a problem he wanted to talk over with someone, he phoned Jason. The two of them had been a support system for one another for years.

This time however when it came to contacting his brothers, Rich opted for Paul. Paul had been married nearly five years; surely in all that time he'd gleaned some perspective on dealing with the opposite sex.

Rich stood and closed his office door before sitting back down and reaching for his phone. Paul worked for the largest of the two Seattle newspapers and was often in the field. Rich felt fortunate when his brother answered the phone.

"Have you got a minute?"

"Sure," Paul teased. "The only thing I've got pressing is a three o'clock deadline."

Since it was a quarter to three, Rich figured he'd better talk fast. "I take it Jason told you about Jamie and me?"

"Not exactly," Paul said, his amusement evident in his voice, "but I was able to put two and two together. Jason confirmed my suspicions, although I have to admit I never suspected you'd agree to allowing Jamie to be artificially inseminated."

"It didn't work out that way."

"That's what Jason said."

Rich could picture his brother in the middle of the newsroom, leaning back in his captain's chair wearing that cocky know-it-all grin of his.

"What can I do for you, little brother?"

"Explain something to me."

"I will if I can," Paul agreed.

"Women."

Paul responded with a low laugh. "You want me to explain a woman's mind. I hope you're kidding? No one, at least no man, will ever be able to understand the way a woman thinks. Trust me, I've got five years more experience in this marriage business. If you don't believe me, ask Dad. He'll tell you the same thing. Take Diane...please." He paused long enough to laugh at his own sorry joke. "She wants another baby. Apparently she isn't busy enough with Ryan and Ronnie. For weeks on end she's been talking of nothing else. She wants a little girl, she says. Good heavens, the twins run her ragged as it is. Besides there's no guarantee we'd have a girl. We actually had a big fight about it last week."

"And?" Rich didn't mean to pry, but he was curious to know how his brother and his wife settled their disagreements.

"Well, I stood my ground, if that's what you mean. Not that it did much good," he admitted reluctantly. "I absolutely refused to talk about having another child. I tried to appease her. I don't want to sound dictatorial or unreasonable. To my way of thinking we should discuss the prospect next year about this time. That way the twins will be in kindergarten by the time the new baby's born. Planning our family makes sense to me."

"What did Diane say?"

"Nothing." This announcement was followed by a significant pause. "But I should mention, she flushed her birth-control pills down the toilet."

"Is she always this stubborn?"

"It's not just Diane. All women are stubborn. To make matters worse, she wore this sexy little piece of black lace to bed. I tried to ignore her, pretend I didn't see . . . you don't need me to tell you what I could see."

"No, I don't." Rich wasn't keen on having his brother bring up the subject of lovemaking. He still didn't know what to make of Jamie's actions that morning. Had he frightened her, wanting her the way he did? Hell, it hadn't seemed that way to him the night before, but what did he know?

Apparently damn little.

"The thing is, Diane will probably get her way simply because I don't have the strength to fight her. I could give up making love to her, but I'd be the one losing out."

Rich rubbed his hand along the back of his neck. "Does Diane ever say one thing when she means another?"

Paul's laugh was low and abrupt. "All the time. Far be it for a woman to come right out and say what she means. Oh, no, a man's left to guess, and heaven forbid if we should happen to guess wrong."

Rich inhaled a long, slow sigh. Paul was confirming what he already knew. "Remember, when we met with

Mom and Dad, how Jamie casually mentioned I was moving in with her?''

"Yeah."

"It surprised the hell out of me when she brought it up. We'd never said a word about it."

"You mean you don't want to move in with her?"

"Of course I do. For weeks now I've been trying to figure out a way to suggest that very thing. Then when I least suspect it, she invites me to live with her, in front of my family. I was so damned excited it was all I could do not to jump up and do flips across the living room floor."

"So what's the problem?"

It was a logical question and one that Rich couldn't answer. "If I knew that, I wouldn't be phoning you."

"All right," Paul said exhaling sharply. "Start at the beginning."

"I drove home with Jamie last night."

"And?" Paul prompted when Rich didn't immediately continue.

"And I ended up staying the night."

"Everything sounds perfectly fine to me."

"It was until this morning," Rich agreed.

"What happened then?"

Rich wished the hell he knew. "I can't honestly say. The alarm went off and we were cuddling like old married folks, talking about nothing in particular. The next thing I know Jamie's out of the shower, with this towel wrapped around her middle like it was a piece of armor. She wouldn't so much as look at me. I played it cool, gave her some space. Some women are modest— I understand that—so I left her alone.

"Before I know it, she's in the kitchen making herself a lunch like it was the most important thing she's ever done. On accident I happened to step too close to her and she practically threw herself against the counter so there was no possibility we'd touch.'' Rich paused to drag a breath through his oxygen-starved lungs. ''To top everything off, I mention not having a key to her place and she says we should reevaluate my moving in with her.''

''I see,'' Paul muttered.

''What'd I do?''

''Something, that's for damn sure. Think,'' Paul advised. ''You must have said something to set her off.''

''Like what?'' They'd done far more kissing than talking.

''How should I know? I wasn't there. Just think . . . review everything you said.''

''I've already tried that, but I can't come up with a single thing I could have done to warrant this reaction.''

''Then ask her.''

''I can do that?''

''Yeah,'' Paul said, but he didn't sound any too sure. ''It's not the normal procedure because . . . well, you'll learn that soon enough yourself. But if you're honestly in the dark about what went wrong, then asking her is as good a means as any. But if you do, be prepared.''

''For what?''

''To have your ego shredded. When Diane acts the way Jamie is, I know I've committed some base deed. Often, and this is what's so damn confusing, Diane can't even tell me what I did. All she knows is that she's furious with me.''

''She doesn't know?'' Rich could barely believe it.

"It's true. She glares at me like I should be arrested. Then, when I can't stand it anymore, I get up the courage to ask her what I did that was so terrible."

"And?"

"And," Paul added with a deep sigh, "she announces she's still getting in touch with her feelings. It has something to do with being a woman—at least that's what Diane claims. She tried to explain it to me once. I nodded and pretended I understood what she was talking about, but to be honest, it sounded like a bunch of bull to me."

"What did she say?"

Once again Paul sighed. "It has something to do with women's role in society, about being taught never to make a fuss or cause waves."

"I see."

"You do?" Paul rallied. "Hell, explain it to me, then."

"I don't understand it, but I can accept it."

"So what are you going to do?"

Rich hesitated. "What you suggest. Ask her."

"You're a good man, Rich Manning." Paul made it sound as if Rich should be awarded a medal for bravery, or at the very least, a twelve-inch-high trophy.

"Let me know how it goes."

"I will," he promised. After thanking his eldest brother for his advice, Rich replaced the telephone receiver. Paul had made it plain that taking such an action with Jamie would require raw courage. But Rich had to know what he'd done that was so beastly or go insane trying to figure it out.

The rest of the afternoon passed in a blur. Because of the project he was working on for the Defense Department, Rich had to stay late that night. He wasn't pleased about it, but the choice had been taken away from him. Bill Hastings and the others were working overtime, as well. Rich couldn't very well announce that he'd had an argument with his wife and then leave.

At a quarter past six, Rich was still working diligently, when there was a polite knock against his door. He glanced up to find Jamie standing there.

If he'd learned anything in the short time he'd been married, it was that women never did the expected. Rich couldn't believe Jamie was there in his office. Especially after their fight that morning.

"Can I come in?"

"Of course." He stood and gestured toward the chair on the opposite side of his desk. Once she sat down, he did, too. Since she was the one who'd come to see him, Rich figured he'd let her do the talking. Hoping to appear as nonchalant as possible, he leaned back in his chair and crossed his long legs.

"I want to apologize for this morning," she said in a small voice.

"No problem." Rich was in a generous mood. Apparently she'd seen the error of her ways, as well she should, and had come to make amends.

"I . . . I was completely unreasonable."

"Does this mean you want me to move in with you after all?"

"Yes, of course . . . that is, if you're still willing."

Was he ever! "It's certainly something to think about," he said evenly. Then, because he was in a generous mood, he added, "I read that a woman is often unreasonable during pregnancy."

"The book said that?" Jamie asked, frowning.

"Something along those lines."

"I see." She opened her purse and reached for her wallet, snapping open the slot meant to store loose change. "I had a key made for you on my lunch hour," she explained, handing it to him.

"I'm working late this evening." He said this hoping she'd suggest he drop in at her place—at *their* place on his way home.

"I figured you would be...that's the reason I stopped off here first."

A short uncomfortable silence passed. Rich figured he should let sleeping dogs lie in regards to what had troubled her earlier in the day. If she'd wanted to tell him, now was the perfect opportunity. More than likely, this was one of those times Paul had mentioned. Jamie probably didn't even know herself and regretted having made such a fuss. At least she was willing to admit she was wrong, which is something a lot of women wouldn't.

"I was thinking I'd bring some of my clothes over this evening," Rich said, hoping she'd offer him some encouragement, let him know how eager she was for him to live with her.

"That would be fine."

"I'll contact Jason and see if he can help me move the furniture and the large items this weekend." He'd put what he didn't need into storage.

"I'll make sure there's plenty of room for your things." Jamie reluctantly stood. "I guess I'll be leaving, then."

"One last thing."

"Sure."

When Rich arrived at her place he didn't want to play any guessing games about their sleeping arrangements. "Where will I be sleeping?"

Jamie's eyes widened at the directness of his question. "Ah . . . that's up to you."

"No, it's not," he returned firmly. "It's completely up to you."

"Anyplace you'd like," she offered almost flippantly.

Rich wasn't going to let it past that easily. "Where would you like me to sleep?"

She hesitated, then lowered her gaze. "With me."

It was as though he'd scaled the gates of heaven and was free to walk through the halls of paradise to have Jamie admit she wanted him in her bed.

"There isn't anyplace else I'd rather sleep," he added. He stood and walked toward her, slipping his arm around her shoulders. The elevator was down the narrow hallway. Rich walked with her. He pushed the button and while they waited, he leaned forward and gently kissed her. The kiss was a reward of sorts. It couldn't have been easy for her to come to him like this, to admit she was wrong.

As so often happened when he kissed her, Rich felt himself wanting more. Much more. She braced her hands against his chest and her touch branded him. A warmth filled his heart and seemed to radiate outward.

When they broke off the kiss, Rich was pleased to note that Jamie was trembling. For that matter, so was he.

"You make me forget," she said in a husky whisper.

Rich understood. She made him forget where he was, as well.

Bill Hastings strolled by and smiled affectionately toward them. He paused, apparently waiting to talk to Rich.

The elevator arrived and although Rich was reluctant to let her go, he still had another hour of paperwork to finish.

"Goodbye, darling," Rich said. "I won't be more than a couple of hours."

Jamie's reaction was instantaneous. She stepped into the elevator and whirled around to face him. Her eyes, her beautiful dark eyes, were spitting fire. At the same time they were brimming with tears.

"That's the most awful thing you've ever said to me, Rich Manning."

Rich was so mystified by her irrational behavior that it took him a moment to respond. "What I said? What did I say?"

"You very well know." With that, the thick elevator doors glided shut.

Chapter Fourteen

"What'd I say?" Rich asked, utterly bewildered. He turned to his coworker at a loss to understand what he'd done that was so terribly wrong.

Bill Hastings's blank look confirmed he was as much in the dark as Rich himself.

"Whatever it was must have been awful. It looked like Jamie was close to tears."

"I don't even know what I did," Rich continued, baffled. Already he felt guilty, and he hadn't a clue what he'd done that was so terrible.

"Maybe she's upset because you told her you wouldn't be home for a couple of hours."

Rich scratched the side of his head. "Maybe so." Although his working overtime had never seemed to trouble Jamie before. At least not that he was aware. Sighing with frustration, Rich decided to give up trying to figure out his wife. Jamie had been a whole lot easier to understand before he married her.

"Leave now," Bill urged, "settle matters with her before it's too late." That meant Rich's coworker would take on the brunt of the paperwork himself and to Rich's way of thinking, that wouldn't be fair.

Rich considered it, then shook his head. "I'll sort matters out with her later."

"You're sure?"

"Positive."

Bill hesitated. "Maybe you should reconsider?" Bill gave him a look that reminded Rich his friend was divorced. It went without saying that Bill wished his circumstances were different. His eyes contained a spark of regret, a spark of concern, as if to suggest if he had it to do over again, he'd work damn hard to save his marriage.

Rich's heart was racing. "You're sure you don't mind?"

"Not in the least. Go. Do what you have to before everything gets blown out of proportion."

"Thanks," Rich said over his shoulder, the urge to hurry dictating his actions. "I owe you one for this."

"Don't mention it . . . only, Rich?"

"Yeah."

"Be happy."

Rich nodded. "I intend to, even if it kills me." At the furious glare Jamie had sent his way, it probably would, too.

Although he hurried out of the building and toward the guest parking, Rich missed her. Jamie's car was nowhere in sight. He released a breath of abject frustration and slapped his hands against the sides of his legs before turning and walking to the employee parking area.

Maybe it was best that he didn't catch her. His mood wasn't the best. Would married life always be this difficult? he wondered. Would his life consist of continually making amends for some imagined wrong? Must he constantly be on his guard, afraid to speak his mind? If that was the case, then the hell with it.

If there'd been something handy to punch, Rich would have done it. Plowing his fist into empty space only served to discourage him more.

How fitting. Fighting imaginary ghosts was how his entire marriage had gone.

Jamie had always been a sensible woman, or she had been until she'd become pregnant. He'd read pregnant women were sometimes temperamental, but this was ridiculous.

Jamie felt like such a fool. Tears marked moist, crooked trails down her cheeks. She wasn't a woman given easily to such blatant emotion. Her actions surprised her even more than they did Rich.

Damn it all, he deserved it. Calling her darling in front of his friend, putting on a big show, pretending to love her. Saying it wasn't sin enough, he had to go and wear a besotted look, as though parting was such sweet sorrow.

Jamie knew it was all a game with him, and she couldn't bear to play any longer. If it was the first time, she might have been able to overlook it, but this nonsense had become a habit of late. When they'd gone to visit his parents, Rich had sat with her at his side, his hand clenching hers. The tender look in his eyes, the way he'd smiled down on her as though the sun rose and set in her face, was more than she could bear.

It was all so hypocritical. Counterfeit love.

When would she ever learn? Men were fickle creatures not to be trusted. She knew Rich, probably better than she did any other man she'd ever dated. His games surprised her. More than that, they hurt her.

Driving and crying didn't make for a safe combination and Jamie slowed down at a red light, brought a tissue out of her purse and loudly blew her nose. After she could see clearly again, she sniffled and continued driving.

Once she was home, she wandered around her empty condo, walking from room to room, wondering if she'd ever be able to erase Rich's presence. It was almost as if she expected him to walk in at any minute. A part of her longed to shoo him out of her life, chase him away by militantly waving a broom, demanding he leave her alone.

Another part of her hungered to run and greet him with open arms.

"This is what happens to you when you fall in love," she chastised herself loudly. She pressed her hand over her smooth, flat stomach and a soft, delicate smile settled over her lips.

Matters were different this time because a child was involved. This time she would walk away from the relationship with a bonus. A very special bonus.

Making herself a cup of tea, Jamie sat in her kitchen nursing her hot drink and her wounded heart. The pile of damp tissues had peaked and she'd composed herself enough to realize her display of anger had been out of character. No doubt Rich had viewed it as completely irrational. When she spoke to him again, she fully intended to set the matter straight.

Pretense was unacceptable and she'd make sure Rich understood that. Damn sure.

A noise came from her front door. Since Jamie routinely kept it locked, she was surprised to hear the latch slip free. A moment later, the door swung open and Rich, standing tall and ominous, entered her condo. One brief glance at the dark, brooding look shining from his eyes, the tightly clenched jaw, told her he was in a dangerous mood. He was furious and he wasn't bothering to hide it.

The first thing Jamie noticed, standing as she was in the doorway leading to the kitchen, was the suitcase he carried with him. It was large and bulky, the kind one would take on an extended vacation. A three-week European tour. A two-week cruise. No one would confuse it with an overnight bag.

He set the luggage piece down with a thud and headed toward her. Wide-eyed, Jamie moved out of his way.

"What are you doing here?" She sounded a whole lot braver than she felt. A challenge wasn't the best way to start their conversation, but it was a beginning. It also told him she refused to be intimidated. He could rant and rave and thunder all he wanted, but she refused to be browbeaten.

"I'm here because I happen to live here." He said it with enough conviction to make the windows vibrate. "Furthermore, I'll be sleeping in the master bedroom with you at my side. Is that understood?"

Coward that she was, Jamie nodded. She wasn't sure she'd ever seen Rich like this. Generally, he treated every situation as though it were a joking matter. He could bluff, cajole and tease himself through just about anything. Jamie already knew what he'd be like when she was in labor. He'd be at her side telling jokes, entertaining the nurses, sharing good-ole-boy jokes with Dr. Fullerton.

"No arguments?" He sounded surprised she wasn't going to fight him over the issue of him living with her, sleeping with her.

Jamie shook her head.

"Good." He nodded once as if to say this was going to be much easier than he'd anticipated. "Now kindly explain what it was that I said that was so despicable, when you left my office."

Jamie found it difficult to speak. "Darling."

"Yes?"

"You called me darling," she said, hating having to explain it. She knotted her fists at her side, her long nails digging deep into the tender flesh of her palms.

"So?" He frowned, genuinely bewildered.

"So... I'd rather you didn't." A lump the size of a cantaloupe was forming in her throat, but Jamie chose to overlook how difficult it was to breathe.

Rich stalked to the far end of her kitchen, his back to her. He braced his hands against the sink, and hung his head as if her words demanded deep concentration. After a moment he turned to face her. "You're sure it doesn't have anything to do with me working overtime?"

"Of course not," Jamie explained, pleasantly surprised to sound so composed. "That would be unreasonable."

"And objecting to me calling you darling isn't?" he stressed, his eyes growing round and wide. His jaw was tight as though he were clenching his teeth to keep from saying something more.

Jamie lowered her gaze to the polished kitchen floor. "I...wouldn't care if you'd meant it. But we both know you didn't and even worse than that..."

"Worse? You mean there's something worse than calling one's wife 'darling'? Does the FBI know about this?"

"Being cute isn't going to help you this time, Rich Manning." She knew it would be impossible to talk to him. He turned everything around to suit himself.

"All right," he said, his voice lower by several decibels. "Tell me what other horrible felony I've committed."

"It was the look you had." To illustrate her point, she crossed her eyes and let her tongue dangle from the corner of her mouth.

"I looked like that?" he challenged disbelievingly. "Don't be ridiculous."

"Not exactly like that, but close enough." She held herself stiff. An unyielding fortress of strength, held together with pride and love.

"What's that supposed to be?"

"You with a besotted look."

He gave a short, abrupt laugh. "Very funny."

"I wasn't trying to be cute."

"I never looked like that in my life." Rich walked over to the round oak table and frowned when he noted the tall pile of tissues. "You've been crying?"

"I...I have a cold."

He flung her a look of disbelief. "I thought you swore you were never going to cry over another man."

"I...I didn't intend to.... I probably wouldn't, either, but I happen to be pregnant and my hormones are all screwed up, so don't take it personally."

"What's happened to us?" He advanced several steps toward her, stopping just short of taking her in his arms. "Jamie, love..."

"Don't say that," she cried, her voice rising to near hysterical levels. Having him call her his love was like pouring alcohol over a cut. It hurt enough to cause her to wince.

"Say what?" He raised his hands, palms upward in sheer frustration.

"Don't call me your love."

"Why the hell not?" he demanded.

"Because I'm not."

"What do you mean?" Rich glared at her, his brow condensed in a thick frown.

"You don't love me and I...I can't tolerate it when you pretend you do." The words vehemently poured out of her until she was shouting, shaking with the force of her anger.

"I love you."

"Oh...right." She wouldn't have believed Rich would lie to her about something so serious. It cut deep against the grain of her pride that he would try to pass off for the truth what she knew to be false.

"You mean you honestly didn't know?" He advanced a few steps, but for every one he took, Jamie retreated two.

"Because it isn't true!"

"How can you say that after the other night?"

"Don't confuse good sex with love." Jamie didn't know what made her say such terrible things, but she couldn't make herself stop. She wore her pride like a protective armor. She'd been hurt so many times before. Her trust had been raped, her heart bruised. She couldn't bear to go through it all again, especially with

Rich, whom she loved so desperately. It was far better for him to believe she didn't care.

"So that's all it was to you . . . good sex?"

"Yes, of course. You don't believe it was anything more, do you?"

With each word she threw at him, his anger increased until it flashed like fire from his eyes.

Jamie's back was flattened against the wall, her fingers splayed against the rough texture as if they would securely hold her in place. She longed to tell him their times together had been the most beautiful, the most meaningful of her life, but she hadn't the strength.

She'd never realized how draining it was to lie.

"I suppose you want me to prove it," he said with such force the wall seemed to vibrate behind her.

"Yes," Jamie returned flippantly, knowing it was an impossible task.

Without looking at her Rich marched past her with long, purpose-filled strides. Jamie was convinced Sherman on his march to the sea couldn't have walked with more determination. He slammed his suitcase onto the floor, opened it and dug through his clothes until he found what he wanted. It looked like a plain white business envelope to Jamie, but she hadn't a clue what it contained.

Without a word he stepped over to her fireplace, reached for a long-stemmed match she kept on the mantle and struck it against the brick. The flame flared eagerly to life. Cupping his hand over the delicate fire, Rich knelt and held the match to the white envelope and set it on the grate. Within seconds the paper was nothing more than charred ashes.

At first Jamie didn't understand the significance of what he was doing. It came to her gradually until each breath she drew became more painful. Rich had burned the marriage agreement they'd had drawn up before the wedding. The one they'd both signed and had notarized.

The tears that had crowded her throat for so long refused to be contained any longer. They sprang to her eyes, burning, smarting. Her throat ached with the need to breathe, sobs crowded one another in their eagerness to escape.

She must have made some slight sound because Rich, whose back was to her, turned slowly. His eyes slid deeply to hers, until Jamie thought she would drown in those blue depths.

Emotions scored her.

Dare she believe? Dare she hope that what he'd said was true and that he did indeed love her? Hope was such a fragile commodity in her eyes. Delicate and easily shattered.

Dare she believe?

Love had always been so painful for her. Disappointing. It had stripped her of her pride, deprived her soul of her aspirations. Cheated her.

Dare she trust her heart again?

It had been so unreliable in the past, leading her down a primrose path and then deserting her in a field of thorns, leaving her scared and weary.

"I'm not interested in a marriage of convenience with you any longer, Jamie," he stated evenly. "I haven't been, since the night I found you with Floyd what's-his-face. I realized then I love you and probably have for years, only I'd been too blind to realize it. Condemn me if you will, but it's the God's honest truth."

Jamie's fragile heart quickened. Tears streamed down her face and she pressed her fingertips to her lips, knowing it would be impossible to speak. Instead, she held out her hand to him, her shoulders trembling with emotion.

Rich moved with the speed of light, hauling her into his arms. His mouth unerringly found hers, and he rained down warm, moist kisses against her quivering mouth. Tender kisses. Fevered kisses.

"I hope to God all this emotion means what I think," he murmured against the delicate curve of her neck.

Jamie's tears fell without restraint. The emotions that boiled within her were too primitive, rooted too deep within her heart to allow her the luxury of answering him with words. Her hands framed his face as she spread eager kisses wherever she could. Desperately she tried to convey everything in her heart, an impossible task at the moment. She cherished him with her lips, kissing him again and again until they both trembled with passion.

"Jamie..." Rich tore his mouth from hers and stared down into her face. He smeared the moisture across the high arch of her cheek with the thick pad of his thumb as his gaze searched hers.

"I love you," she managed in a breathless whisper.

His smile was more brilliant than a rainbow after the fiercest storm. "I know." He wore a cocky grin as he swung her effortlessly into his arms and walked purposely toward the master bedroom.

Tenderly he pressed her against the mattress and moved over her. When he kissed her, their passion flared to life like a jet engine ready to roar off a runway. Two eager souls ready to soar in the security of their love.

"Tell me what you said wasn't true," he pleaded. "Tell me our lovemaking touched you the same as it did me."

Jamie tried to answer him with words, reassure him it had been her pain talking, her disillusionment with love, but she couldn't speak for the knot in her throat. Smiling, she gazed up at him, allowing all the love in her heart to spill into her eyes. She wrapped her arms around his neck and kissed him.

They made love gently, slowly and when they finished, they held each other. For a long time neither spoke. Words weren't necessary. Not when their hearts were so full.

They kissed after a while and Rich rolled onto his back, taking her with him. Her soft belly was flush with his own. Tenderly his hand caressed the small of her back.

"I love you," he whispered. "I love our baby, too."

"I know... I'm sorry I doubted."

Content, Jamie nestled against him, pressing her ear to his heart, which beat solidly against his chest. Her own heart was heavy with emotion. Such strong, vital emotion. She'd thought to close herself off from love, but Rich had made that impossible.

His hand reached for hers. Palm to palm. Tomorrow to tomorrow. Contentment to contentment.

Epilogue

The brightly decorated Christmas tree was nestled in the corner of Rich and Jamie's spacious living room, tucked in front of a large bay window that overlooked Puget Sound.

Jamie sat with her swollen ankles elevated on the ottoman while Rich brought her in a cup of hot tea from the kitchen. He'd insisted upon doing dishes and Jamie hadn't put up much of an argument. She was tired and crabby and impatient for their baby to be born.

"We really should take down the tree," she said, feeling slightly guilty that it was still there when Christmas had passed several days before.

"Take down the tree," Rich objected. "We can't do that!"

"Why not?"

"Junior wants to see it."

"Rich," Jamie muttered, her hands resting on her protruding stomach. "I've got news for you. Junior has decided he'd rather not be born. He's hooked his foot over my ribs and claims he'd rather stay right where he is."

"You're only three days past your due date."

"It feels like three months." She'd given up viewing her feet months earlier. She'd also given up arguing with Rich over the sex of their child. He absolutely insisted it was a boy. It was a matter of Manning family pride. Paul's twins were boys and then Taylor had complicated everything by having a son first. It was tradition, Rich explained.

The Mannings had always been big on tradition.

The only big thing at the moment, however, was Jamie. She felt as graceful as a semitruck and as awkward as a one-legged kangaroo.

"Can I get you anything more?" Rich asked. "A pillow? Your knitting? A book to read?"

"Stop being so solicitous," she snapped.

"My, my, are we a bit testy this evening?"

"Don't be cute, either. I'm not in the mood for cute."

"How about adoring?"

"Maybe…but you're going to have to convince me."

"Perhaps I should try for the besotted look." He crossed his eyes and dangled his tongue out of the side of his mouth, imitating the impression she'd done of him months earlier.

Despite her low spirits, Jamie laughed and held her arms out to him. "I love you, even if you do look like a goose."

Rich sat on the ottoman facing her. "I love you, too. I must, otherwise I wouldn't be this worried." The humor drained from his eyes as he leaned forward and pressed his hand over her stomach. "Come out, come out whoever you are."

"Are you really concerned?" He hid his anxiety behind a teasing facade, Jamie realized. She'd been so wrapped up in her own apprehensions that she hadn't taken the time to address Rich's.

"I'm anxious." His hands gripped hers and he raised her knuckles to his mouth and gently kissed her fingers.

"So am I! I want this baby to be born."

"It's amazing to me how much I love him already," Rich whispered, his eyes growing serious. "At first, the baby was something we talked about. When I learned you were pregnant I was so excited I could have walked on water. We talked about him all the time, planned our lives around him. Within a few weeks of learning you were pregnant, we were living together, then we sold your condo and moved here. That was only the beginning of all the changes that have taken place in our lives."

"I know."

"Then Junior started getting sassy, moving about, letting us know he was there."

"He's convinced me he'll do exceptionally well in kick ball."

"I'll never forget the first time I felt him move."

"I won't, either," Jamie muttered. "We were making love."

"He was just saying hello, letting us know he was there."

"Frankly, I found it a bit disconcerting," Jamie said, having a difficult time containing a laugh.

Rich smiled that cocky, lopsided grin of his that never failed to disarm her. "Everything's changed in the past month.'' Once again his blue eyes brightened. ''I realized this child was more than an elbow against his mother's ribs. He was a part of you and me—the very best part of us both. I know it sounds silly, but every time I think about him, I get all soft inside. I want to hold him in my arms and tell him how much his mother and I wanted him. Enough to go to exorbitant measures.''

''Not that it was necessary,'' Jamie whispered. ''Might I remind you Junior was conceived in the good old-fashioned way.''

Rich leaned forward and reminded her of some of the other good old-fashioned methods they'd discovered in the past several months. She was laughing when she felt the first contraction. Her eyes widened and she squeezed Rich's hand.

''Jamie?''

''I think all my complaining might have done some good. Have you got the watch?''

Rich paled, nodded, then rushed into their bedroom, returning with the stopwatch he'd purchased after attending the Lamaze classes.

He knelt before her, clasping her hand in his own. ''Are you ready, my love?''

Jamie grinned and nodded. She'd been ready for this moment for nine long months.

With a loud squall, Bethany Marie Manning made her way into the world thirteen hours later. Rich was at Jamie's side in the delivery room. When Dr. Fullerton announced they had a daughter, Rich looked to Jamie, his face filled with wonder and surprise.

''She's a girl?'' he asked, as though he wasn't sure he'd heard correctly.

"Do you want to check for yourself?" Dr. Fullerton teased.

Jamie watched her husband, searching for any signs of disappointment, but if there were any she didn't see them. The nurse weighed Bethany, and then wrapped the protesting infant in a warm blanket and handed her to Rich.

Rich stared down at the bright pink face and smiled. When he looked over to Jamie his eyes shone with unshed tears. "She's beautiful."

"You're not disappointed?"

"Are you crazy? I always wanted a daughter. I just said I wanted a boy to keep you off guard." Very gently, Rich bent down and kissed his child's forehead.

Hours later, Jamie stirred in her hospital bed and noticed Rich was asleep in the chair next to her. His head was resting against the side of her head. Smiling contentedly to herself, she rubbed her fingers through his tangled hair.

Yawning, Rich raised his head. "Hello, little mother."

"Hello, proud daddy."

"She is so beautiful. Oh, Jamie, I can't believe how much I love her. And you." He kissed her hand and then placed it against his jaw, holding it in place. "I never knew I could feel like this."

Feeling dreamy and tired, Jamie nodded and closed her eyes.

"Don't you worry about a thing," Rich whispered, his face close to hers. "I've taken care of everything."

Jamie's eyes flew open. "What do you mean by that?"

"Ballet classes." He pulled open the drawer to the bedside table and withdrew a thick Seattle phone book. "I've contacted two schools, both of whom are sending out brochures. I also talked to a teacher about piano lessons."

"Rich!"

"Just kidding," he joked. He lifted her hand and pressed it between his own. "I love you so much, Jamie." Something close to worship shone in his eyes.

They had come so far, Jamie mused. Life had taught them each a valuable lesson. They'd thought to manipulate fate, create their own destiny.

Instead, love had caught them unaware.

*   *   *   *   *

NORA ROBERTS

Love has a language all its own, and for centuries, flowers have symbolized love's finest expression. Discover the language of flowers—and love—in this romantic collection of 48 favorite books by bestselling author Nora Roberts.

Starting in February, two titles will be available each month at your favorite retail outlet.

In March, look for:

Irish Rose, Volume #3
Storm Warning, Volume #4

In April, look for:

First Impressions, Volume #5
Reflections, Volume #6

Collect all 48 titles and become fluent in

THE LANGUAGE of LOVE

Silhouette Special Edition®

salutes

MOMENTS OF GLORY

from Lindsay McKenna

In a country torn with conflict, in a time of bitter passions, these brave men and women wage a war against all odds... and a timeless battle for honor, for fleeting moments of glory, for the promise of enduring love.

February: RIDE THE TIGER (#721) Survivor Dany Villard is wise to the love-'em-and-leave-'em ways of war, but wounded hero Gib Ramsey swears she's captured his heart... forever.

March: ONE MAN'S WAR (#727) The war raging inside brash and bold Captain Pete Mallory threatens to destroy him, until Tess Ramsey's tender love guides him toward peace.

April: OFF LIMITS (#733) Soft-spoken Marine Jim McKenzie saved Alexandra Vance's life in Vietnam; now he needs her love to save his honor....

To order the first MOMENTS OF GLORY title, RIDE THE TIGER (SE #721), please send your name, address, zip or postal code, along with a check or money order for $3.29 (please do not send cash), plus 75¢ postage and handling ($1.00 in Canada), payable to Silhouette Reader Service to:

In the U.S.
3010 Walden Avenue
P.O. Box 1396
Buffalo, NY 14269-1396

In Canada
P.O. Box 609
Fort Erie, Ontario
L2A 5X3

Please specify book title with your order.
Canadian residents add applicable federal and provincial taxes.

Take 4 bestselling love stories FREE

Plus get a FREE surprise gift!

From the popular author of the bestselling title
DUNCAN'S BRIDE (Intimate Moments #349)
comes the

LINDA
HOWARD
COLLECTION

Two exquisite collector's editions that contain four of
Linda Howard's early passionate love stories. To add
these special volumes to your own library, be sure
to look for:

VOLUME ONE: *Midnight Rainbow*
Diamond Bay
(Available in March)

VOLUME TWO: *Heartbreaker*
White Lies
(Available in April)

SLH92